W9-CAD-896

THE STRENGTH OF GIDEON

And Other Stories: Expanded Edition

THE STRENGTH OF GIDEON

And Other Stories: Expanded Edition

PAUL LAURENCE DUNBAR

WILDSIDE PRESS

THE STRENGTH OF GIDEON AND OTHER STORIES:
EXPANDED EDITION

This edition published 2005 by Wildside Press, LLC.
www.wildsidepress.com

TO MY GOOD FRIEND AND TEACHER
CAPTAIN CHARLES B. STIVERS

CONTENTS

THE STRENGTH OF GIDEON

Old Mam' Henry, and her word may be taken, said that it was "De powerfulles' sehmont she ever had hyeahd in all huh bo'n days." That was saying a good deal, for the old woman had lived many years on the Stone place and had heard many sermons from preachers, white and black. She was a judge, too.

It really must have been a powerful sermon that Brother Lucius preached, for Aunt Doshy Scott had fallen in a trance in the middle of the aisle, while "Merlatter Mag," who was famed all over the place for having white folk's religion and never "waking up," had broken through her reserve and shouted all over the camp ground.

Several times Cassie had shown signs of giving way, but because she was frail some of the solicitous sisters held her with self-congratulatory care, relieving each other now and then, that each might have a turn in the rejoicings. But as the preacher waded out deeper and deeper into the spiritual stream, Cassie's efforts to make her feelings known became more and more decided. He told them how the spears of the Midianites had "clashed upon de shiels of de Gideonites, an' aftah while, wid de powah of de Lawd behin' him, de man Gideon triumphed mightily," and swaying then and wailing in the dark woods, with grim branches waving in the breath of their own excitement, they could hear above the tumult the clamor of the fight, the clashing of the spears, and the ringing of the shields. They could see the conqueror coming home in triumph. Then when he cried, "A-who, I say, a-who is in Gideon's ahmy today?" and the wailing chorus took up the note, "A-who!" it was too much even for frail Cassie, and, deserted by the solicitous sisters, in the words of Mam' Henry, "she broke a-loose, and faihly tuk de place."

Gideon had certainly triumphed, and when a little boy baby came to Cassie two or three days later, she named him Gideon in honor of the great Hebrew warrior whose story had so wrought upon her. All the plantation knew the spiritual significance of the name, and from the day of his birth the child was as one set apart to a holy mission on earth.

Say what you will of the influences which the circumstances surrounding birth have upon a child, upon this one at least the effect was unmistakable. Even as a baby he seemed to realize the weight of responsibility which had been laid upon his little black shoulders, and there was a complacent dignity in the very way in which he drew upon the sweets of his dirty sugar-teat when the maternal breast was far off bending over the sheaves of the field.

He was a child early destined to sacrifice and self-effacement, and as he grew older and other youngsters came to fill Cassie's cabin, he took up his lot with the meekness of an infantile Moses. Like a Moses he was, too, leading his little flock to the promised land, when he grew to the age at which, barefooted and one-shifted, he led or carried his little brothers and sisters about the quarters. But the "promised land" never took him into the direction of the stables, where the other pickaninnies worried the horses, or into the region of the hen-coops, where egg-sucking was a common crime.

No boy ever rolled or tumbled in the dirt with a heartier glee than did Gideon, but no warrior, not even his illustrious prototype himself, ever kept sterner discipline in his ranks when his followers seemed prone to overstep the bounds of right. At a very early age his shrill voice could be heard calling in admonitory tones, caught from his mother's very lips, "You 'Nelius, don' you let me ketch you th'owin' at ol' mis' guinea-hens no mo'; you hyeah me?" or "Hi'am, you come offen de top er dat shed 'fo' you fall an' brek yo' naik all to pieces."

It was a common sight in the evening to see him sitting upon the low rail fence which ran before the quarters, his shift blowing in the wind, and his black legs lean and bony against the whitewashed rails, as he swayed to and fro, rocking and singing one of his numerous brothers to sleep, and always his song was of war and victory, albeit crooned in a low, soothing voice. Sometimes it was "Turn Back Pharaoh's Army," at others "Jinin' Gideon's Band." The latter was a favorite, for he seemed to have a proprietary interest in it, although, despite the martial inspiration of his name, "Gideon's band" to him meant an aggregation of people with horns and fiddles.

Steve, who was Cassie's man, declared that he had never seen such a child, and, being quite as religious as Cassie herself, early began to talk Scripture and religion to the boy. He was aided in this when his master, Dudley Stone, a man of the faith, began a little Sunday class for the religiously inclined of the quarters, where the old familiar stories were told in simple language to the slaves and explained. At these meetings Gideon became a shining light. No one listened more eagerly to the teacher's words, or more readily answered his questions at review. No one was wider-mouthed or whiter-eyed. His admonitions to his family now took on a different complexion, and he could be heard calling across a lot to a mischievous sister, "Bettah tek keer daih, Lucy Jane, Gawd's a-watchin' you; bettah tek keer."

The appointed man is always marked, and so Gideon was by always receiving his full name. No one ever shortened his scriptural appellation into Gid. He was always Gideon from the time he bore the name out of the heat of camp-meeting fervor until his master discovered his worthiness and filled Cassie's breast with pride by taking him into the house to learn "mannahs and 'po'tment."

As a house servant he was beyond reproach, and next to his religion his Mas' Dudley and Miss Ellen claimed his devotion and fidelity. The young mistress and young master learned to depend fearlessly upon his faithfulness.

It was good to hear old Dudley Stone going through the house in a mock fury, crying, "Well, I never saw such a house; it seems as if there isn't a soul in it that can do without Gideon. Here I've got him up here to wait on me, and it's Gideon here and Gideon there, and every time I turn around some of you have sneaked him off. Gideon, come here!" And the black boy smiled and came.

But all his days were not days devoted to men's service, for there came a time when love claimed him for her own, when the clouds took on a new color, when the sough of the wind was music in his ears, and he saw heaven in Martha's eyes. It all came about in this way.

Gideon was young when he got religion and joined the church, and he grew up strong in the faith. Almost by the time he had become a valuable house servant he had grown to be an invaluable servant of the Lord. He had a good, clear voice that could lead a hymn out of all the labyrinthian wanderings of an ignorant congregation, even when he had to improvise both words and music; and he was a mighty man of prayer. It was thus he met Martha. Martha was brown and buxom and comely, and her rich contralto voice was loud and high on the sisters' side in meeting time. It was the voices that did it at first. There was no hymn or "spiritual" that Gideon could start to which Martha could not sing an easy blending second, and never did she open a tune that Gideon did not swing into it with a wonderfully sweet, flowing, natural bass. Often he did not know the piece, but that did not matter, he sang anyway. Perhaps when they were out he would go to her and ask, "Sis' Martha, what was that hymn you stahrted today?" and she would probably answer, "Oh, dat was jes' one o' my mammy's ol' songs."

"Well, it sholy was mighty pretty. Indeed it was."

"Oh, thanky, Brothah Gidjon, thanky."

Then a little later they began to walk back to the master's house together, for Martha, too, was one of the favored ones, and served, not in the field, but in the big house.

The old women looked on and conversed in whispers about the pair, for they were wise, and what their old eyes saw, they saw.

"Oomph," said Mam' Henry, for she commented on everything, "dem too is jes' natchelly singin' demse'ves togeddah."

"Dey's lak de mo'nin' stahs," interjected Aunt Sophy.

"How 'bout dat?" sniffed the older woman, for she objected to any one's alluding to subjects she did not understand.

"Why, Mam' Henry, ain' you nevah hyeahd tell o' de mo'nin' stahs whut sung deyse'ves togeddah?"

"No, I ain't, an' I been livin' a mighty sight longah'n you, too. I knows all 'bout when de stahs fell, but dey ain' nevah done no singin' dat I knows 'bout."

"Do heish, Mam' Henry, you sho' su'prises me. W'y, dat ain' happenin's, dat's Scripter."

"Look hyeah, gal, don't you tell me dat's Scripter, an' me been a-settin' undah de Scripter fu' nigh onto sixty yeah."

"Well, Mam' Henry, I may 'a' been mistook, but sho' I took hit fu' Scripter. Mebbe de preachah I hyeahd was jes' inlinin'."

"Well, wheddah hit's Scripter er not, dey's one t'ing su'tain, I tell you, — dem two is singin' deyse'ves togeddah."

"Hit's a fac', an' I believe it."

"An' it's a mighty good thing, too. Brothah Gidjon is de nicest house dahky dat I ever hyeahd tell on. Dey jes' de same diffunce 'twixt him an' de othah houseboys as dey is 'tween real quality an' strainers — he got mannahs, but he ain't got aihs."

"Heish, ain't you right!"

"An' while de res' of dem ain' thinkin' 'bout nothin' but dancin' an' ca'in' on, he makin' his peace, callin', an' 'lection sho'."

"I tell you, Mam' Henry, dey ain' nothin' like a spichul named chile."

"Humph! g'long, gal; 'tain't in de name; de biggest devil I evah knowed was named Moses Aaron. 'Tain't in de name, hit's all in de man hisse'f."

But notwithstanding what the gossips said of him, Gideon went on his way, and knew not that the one great power of earth had taken hold of him until they gave the great party down in the quarters, and he saw Martha in all her glory. Then love spoke to him with no uncertain sound.

It was a dancing-party, and because neither he nor Martha dared countenance dancing, they had strolled away together under the pines that lined the white road, whiter now in the soft moonlight. He had never known the pinecones smell so sweet before in all his life. She had never known just how the moonlight flecked the road before. This was lovers' lane to them. He didn't understand why his heart kept throbbing so furiously, for they were walking slowly, and when a shadow thrown across the road from a by-standing bush frightened her into pressing close up to him, he could not have told why his arm stole round her waist and drew her slim form up to him, or why his lips found hers, as eye looked into eye. For their simple hearts love's mystery was too deep, as it is for wiser ones.

Some few stammering words came to his lips, and she answered the best she could. Then why did the moonlight flood them so, and why were the heavens so full of stars? Out yonder in the black hedge a mocking-bird was singing, and he was translating — oh, so poorly — the song of their hearts. They forgot the dance, they forgot all but their love.

"An' you won't ma'y nobody else but me, Martha?"

"You know I won't, Gidjon."

"But I mus' wait de yeah out?"

"Yes, an' den don't you think Mas' Stone'll let us have a little cabin of ouah own jest outside de quahtahs?"

"Won't it be blessid? Won't it be blessid?" he cried, and then the kindly moon went under a cloud for a moment and came out smiling, for he had peeped through and had seen what passed. Then they walked back hand in hand to the dance along the transfigured road, and they found that the first part of the festivities were over, and all the people had sat down to supper. Every one laughed when they went in. Martha held back and perspired with embarrassment. But even though he saw some of the older heads whispering in a corner, Gideon was not ashamed. A new light was in his eyes, and a new boldness had come to him. He led Martha up to the grinning group, and said in his best singing voice, "Whut you laughin' at? Yes, I's popped de question, an' she says 'Yes,' an' long 'bout a yeah f'om now you kin all 'spec' a' invitation." This was a formal announcement. A shout arose from the happy-go-lucky people, who sorrowed alike in each other's sorrows, and joyed in each other's joys. They sat down at a table, and their health was drunk in cups of cider and persimmon beer.

Over in the corner Mam' Henry mumbled over her pipe, "Wha'd I tell you? wha'd I tell you?" and Aunt Sophy replied, "Hit's de pa'able of de mo'nin' stahs."

"Don't talk to me 'bout no mo'nin' stahs," the mammy snorted; "Gawd jes' fitted dey voices togeddah, an' den j'ined dey hea'ts. De mo'nin' stahs ain't got nothin' to do wid it."

"Mam' Henry," said Aunt Sophy, impressively, "you's a' oldah ooman den I is, an' I ain' sputin' hit; but I say dey done 'filled Scripter 'bout de mo'nin' stahs; dey's done sung deyse'ves togeddah."

The old woman sniffed.

The next Sunday at meeting some one got the start of Gideon, and began a new hymn. It ran:

"At de ma'ige of de Lamb, oh Lawd,
    God done gin His 'sent.
Dey dressed de Lamb all up in white,
    God done gin His 'sent.
Oh, wasn't dat a happy day,
Oh, wasn't dat a happy day, Good Lawd,
Oh, wasn't dat a happy day,
    De ma'ige of de Lamb!"

The wailing minor of the beginning broke into a joyous chorus at the end, and Gideon wept and laughed in turn, for it was his wedding-song.

The young man had a confidential chat with his master the next morning, and the happy secret was revealed.

"What, you scamp!" said Dudley Stone. "Why, you've got even more sense than I gave you credit for; you've picked out the finest girl on the plantation, and the one best suited to you. You couldn't have done better if the match had been made for you. I reckon this must be one of the marriages that are made in heaven. Marry her, yes, and with a preacher. I don't see why you want to wait a year."

Gideon told him his hopes of a near cabin.

"Better still," his master went on; "with you two joined and up near the big house, I'll feel as safe for the folks as if an army was camped around, and, Gideon, my boy," — he put his arms on the black man's shoulders, — "if I should slip away some day —"

The slave looked up, startled.

"I mean if I should die — I'm not going to run off, don't be alarmed — I want you to help your young Mas' Dud look after his mother and Miss Ellen; you hear? Now that's the one promise I ask of you, — come what may, look after the women folks." And the man promised and went away smiling.

His year of engagement, the happiest time of a young man's life, began on golden wings. There came rumors of war, and the wings of the glad-hued year drooped sadly. Sadly they drooped, and seemed to fold, when one day, between the rumors and predictions of strife, Dudley Stone, the old master, slipped quietly away out into the unknown.

There were wife, daughter, son, and faithful slaves about his bed, and they wept for him sincere tears, for he had been a good husband and father and a kind master. But he smiled, and, conscious to the last, whispered to them a cheery good-bye. Then, turning to Gideon, who stood there bowed with grief, he raised one weak finger, and his lips made the word, "Remember!"

They laid him where they had laid one generation after another of the Stones and it seemed as if a pall of sorrow had fallen upon the whole place. Then, still grieving, they turned their long-distracted attention to the things that had been going on around, and lo! the ominous mutterings were loud, and the cloud of war was black above them.

It was on an April morning when the storm broke, and the plantation, master and man, stood dumb with consternation, for they had hoped, they had believed, it would pass. And now there was the buzz of men who talked in secret corners. There were hurried saddlings and feverish rides to town. Somewhere in the quarters was whispered the forbidden word "freedom," and it was taken up and dropped breathlessly from the ends of a hundred tongues. Some of the older ones scouted it, but from some who held young children to their breasts there were deep-souled prayers in the dead of night. Over the meetings in the woods or in the log church a strange reserve brooded, and even the prayers took on a guarded tone. Even from the fulness of their hearts, which longed for liberty, no open word that could offend the mistress or the young master went up to the Almighty. He might know their hearts, but no tongue in meeting gave vent to what was in them, and even Gideon sang no more of the gospel army. He was sad because of this new trouble coming hard upon the heels of the old, and Martha was grieved because he was.

Finally the trips into town budded into something, and on a memorable evening when the sun looked peacefully through the pines, young Dudley Stone rode into the yard dressed in a suit of gray, and on his shoulders were the straps of office. The servants gathered around him with a sort of awe and followed him until he alighted at the porch. Only Mam' Henry, who had been nurse to both him and his sister, dared follow him in. It was a sad scene within, but such a one as any Southern home where there were sons might have shown that awful year. The mother tried to be brave, but her old hands shook, and her tears fell upon her son's brown head, tears of grief at parting, but through which shone the fire of a noble pride. The young Ellen hung about his neck with sobs and caresses.

"Would you have me stay?" he asked her.

"No! no! I know where your place is, but oh, my brother!"

"Ellen," said the mother in a trembling voice, "you are the sister of a soldier now."

The girl dried her tears and drew herself up. "We won't burden your heart, Dudley, with our tears, but we will weight you down with our love and prayers."

It was not so easy with Mam' Henry. Without protest, she took him to her bosom and rocked to and fro, wailing "My baby! my baby!" and the tears that fell from the young man's eyes upon her grey old head cost his manhood nothing.

Gideon was behind the door when his master called him. His sleeve was traveling down from his eyes as he emerged.

"Gideon," said his master, pointing to his uniform, "you know what this means?"

"Yes, suh."

"I wish I could take you along with me. But —"

"Mas' Dud," Gideon threw out his arms in supplication.

"You remember father's charge to you, take care of the women-folks." He took the servant's hand, and, black man and white, they looked into each other's eyes, and the compact was made. Then Gideon gulped and said "Yes, suh" again.

Another boy held the master's horse and rode away behind him when he vaulted into the saddle, and the man of battle-song and warrior name went back to mind the women-folks.

Then began the disintegration of the plantation's population. First Yellow Bob slipped away, and no one pursued him. A few blamed him, but they soon followed as the year rolled away. More were missing every time a Union camp lay near, and great tales were told of the chances for young negroes who would go as body-servants to the Yankee officers. Gideon heard all and was silent.

Then as the time of his marriage drew near he felt a greater strength, for there was one who would be with him to help him keep his promise and his faith.

The spirit of freedom had grown strong in Martha as the days passed, and when her lover went to see her she had strange things to say. Was he going to stay? Was he going to be a slave when freedom and a livelihood lay right within his grasp? Would he keep her a slave? Yes, he would do it all — all.

She asked him to wait.

Another year began, and one day they brought Dudley Stone home to lay beside his father. Then most of the remaining negroes went. There was no master now. The two bereaved women wept, and Gideon forgot that he wore the garb of manhood and wept with them.

Martha came to him.

"Gidjon," she said, "I's waited a long while now. Mos' eve'ybody else is gone. Ain't you goin'?"

"No."

"But, Gidjon, I wants to be free. I know how good dey've been to us; but, oh, I wants to own myse'f. They're talkin' 'bout settin' us free every hour."

"I can wait."

"They's a camp right near here."

"I promised."

"The of'cers wants body-servants, Gidjon —"

"Go, Martha, if you want to, but I stay."

She went away from him, but she or some one else got word to young Captain Jack Griswold of the near camp that there was an excellent servant on the plantation who only needed a little persuading, and he came up to see him.

"Look here," he said, "I want a body-servant. I'll give you ten dollars a month."

"I've got to stay here."

"But, you fool, what have you to gain by staying here?"

"I'm goin' to stay."

"Why, you'll be free in a little while, anyway."

"All right."

"Of all fools," said the Captain. "I'll give you fifteen dollars."

"I do' want it."

"Well, your girl's going, anyway. I don't blame her for leaving such a fool as you are."

Gideon turned and looked at him.

"The camp is going to be moved up on this plantation, and there will be a requisition for this house for officers' quarters, so I'll see you again," and Captain Griswold went his way.

Martha going! Martha going! Gideon could not believe it. He would not. He saw her, and she confirmed it. She was going as an aid to the nurses. He gasped, and went back to mind the women-folks.

They did move the camp up nearer, and Captain Griswold came to see Gideon again, but he could get no word from him, save "I'm goin' to stay," and he went away in disgust, entirely unable to understand such obstinacy, as he called it.

But the slave had his moments alone, when the agony tore at his breast and rended him. Should he stay? The others were going. He would soon be free. Every one had said so, even his mistress one day. Then Martha was going. "Martha! Martha!" his heart called.

The day came when the soldiers were to leave, and he went out sadly to watch them go. All the plantation, that had been white with tents, was dark again, and everywhere were moving, blue-coated figures.

Once more his tempter came to him. "I'll make it twenty dollars," he said, but Gideon shook his head. Then they started. The drums tapped. Away they went, the flag kissing the breeze. Martha stole up to say good-bye to him. Her eyes were overflowing, and she clung to him.

"Come, Gidjon," she plead, "fu' my sake. Oh, my God, won't you come with us — it's freedom." He kissed her, but shook his head.

"Hunt me up when you do come," she said, crying bitterly, "fu' I do love you, Gidjon, but I must go. Out yonder is freedom," and she was gone with them.

He drew out a pace after the troops, and then, turning, looked back at the house. He went a step farther, and then a woman's gentle voice called him, "Gideon!" He stopped. He crushed his cap in his hands, and the tears came into his eyes. Then he answered, "Yes, Mis' Ellen, I's a-comin'."

He stood and watched the dusty column until the last blue leg swung out of sight and over the grey hills the last drum-tap died away, and then turned and retraced his steps toward the house.

Gideon had triumphed mightily.

MAMMY PEGGY'S PRIDE

In the failing light of the midsummer evening, two women sat upon the broad veranda that ran round three sides of the old Virginia mansion. One was young and slender with the slightness of delicate girlhood. The other was old, black and ample, — a typical mammy of the old south. The girl was talking in low, subdued tones touched with a note of sadness that was strange in one of her apparent youth, but which seemed as if somehow in consonance with her sombre garments.

"No, no, Peggy," she was saying, "we have done the best we could, as well as even papa could have expected of us if he had been here. It was of no use to keep struggling and straining along, trying to keep the old place from going, out of a sentiment, which, however honest it might have been, was neither common sense nor practical. Poor people, and we are poor, in spite of the little we got for the place, cannot afford to have feelings. Of course I hate to see strangers take possession of the homestead, and — and — papa's and mamma's and brother Phil's graves are out there on the hillside. It is hard, — hard, but what was I to do? I couldn't plant and hoe and plow, and you couldn't, so I am beaten, beaten." The girl threw out her hands with a despairing gesture and burst into tears.

Mammy Peggy took the brown head in her lap and let her big hands wander softly over the girl's pale face. "Sh, — sh," she said as if she were soothing a baby, "don't go on lak dat. W'y whut's de mattah wid you, Miss Mime? 'Pears lak you done los' all yo' spe'it. Whut you reckon yo' pappy 'u'd t'ink ef he could see you ca'in' on dis away? Didn' he put his han' on yo' haid an' call you his own brave little gal, jes' befo', jes' befo' — he went?"

The girl raised her head for a moment and looked at the old woman.

"Oh, mammy, mammy," she cried, "I have tried so hard to be brave — to be really my father's daughter, but I can't, I can't. Everything I turn my hand to fails. I've tried sewing, but here every one sews for herself now. I've even tried writing," and here a crimson glow burned in her cheeks, "but oh, the awful regularity with which everything came back to me. Why, I even put you in a story, Mammy Peggy, you dear old, good, unselfish thing, and the hard-hearted editor had the temerity to decline you with thanks."

"I wouldn't'a' nevah lef' you nohow, honey."

Mima laughed through her tears. The strength of her first grief had passed, and she was viewing her situation with a whimsical enjoyment of its humorous points.

"I don't know," she went on, "it seems to me that it's only in stories themselves that destitute young Southern girls get on and make fame and fortune with their pens. I'm sure I couldn't."

"Of course you couldn't. Whut else do you 'spect? Whut you know 'bout mekin' a fortune? Ain't you a Ha'ison? De Ha'isons nevah was no buyin' an' sellin', mekin' an' tradin' fambly. Dey was gent'men an' ladies f'om de ve'y fus' beginnin'."

"Oh what a pity one cannot sell one's quality for daily bread, or trade off one's blue blood for black coffee."

"Miss Mime, is you out o' yo' haid?" asked Mammy Peggy in disgust and horror.

"No, I'm not, Mammy Peggy, but I do wish that I could traffic in some of my too numerous and too genteel ancestors instead of being compelled to dispose of my ancestral home and be turned out into the street like a pauper."

"Heish, honey, heish, I can' stan' to hyeah you talk dat-away. I's so'y to see dee ol' place go, but you got to go out of it wid yo' haid up, jes' ez ef you was gwine away fo' a visit an' could come back w'en evah you wanted to."

"I shall slink out of it like a cur. I can't meet the eyes of the new owner; I shall hate him."

"W'y, Miss Mime, whaih's yo' pride? Whaih's yo' Ha'ison pride?"

"Gone, gone with the deed of this house and its furniture. Gone with the money I paid for the new cottage and its cheap chairs."

"Gone, hit ain' gone, fu' ef you won't let on to have it, I will. I'll show dat new man how yo' pa would 'a' did ef he'd 'a' been hyeah."

"What, you, Mammy Peggy?"

"Yes, me, I ain' a-gwine to let him t'ink dat de Ha'isons didn' have no quality."

"Good, mammy, you make me remember who I am, and what my duty is. I shall see Mr. Northcope when he comes, and I'll try to make my Harrison pride sustain me when I give up to him everything I have held dear. Oh, mammy, mammy!"

"Heish, chile, sh, sh, er go on, dat's right, yo' eyes is open now an' you kin cry a little weenty bit. It'll do you good. But when dat new man comes I want mammy's lamb to look at him an' hol' huh haid lak' huh ma used to hol' hern, an' I reckon Mistah No'thcope gwine to withah away."

And so it happened that when Bartley Northcope came the next day to take possession of the old Virginia mansion he was welcomed at the door, and ushered into the broad parlor by Mammy Peggy, stiff and unbending in the faded finery of her family's better days.

"Miss Mime'll be down in a minute," she told him, and as he sat in the great old room, and looked about him at the evidences of ancient affluence, his spirit was subdued by the silent tragedy which his possession of it evinced. But he could not but feel a thrill at the bit of comedy which is on the edge of every tragedy, as he thought of Mammy Peggy and her formal reception. "She let me into my own house," he thought to himself, "with the air of granting me a favor." And then there was a step on the stair; the door opened, and Miss Mima stood before him, proud, cold, white, and beautiful.

He found his feet, and went forward to meet her. "Mr. Northcope," she said, and offered her hand daintily, hesitatingly. He took it, and thought, even in that flash of a second, what a soft, tiny hand it was.

"Yes," he said, "and I have been sitting here, overcome by the vastness of your fine old house."

The "your" was delicate, she thought, but she only said, "Let me help you to recovery with some tea. Mammy will bring some," and then she blushed very red. "My old nurse is the only servant I have with me, and she is always mammy to me." She remembered, and throwing up her proud little head rang for the old woman.

Directly, Mammy Peggy came marching in like a grenadier. She bore a tray with the tea things on it, and after she had set it down hovered in the room as if to chaperon her mistress. Bartley felt decidedly uncomfortable. Mima's manners were all that politeness could require, but he felt as if she resented his coming even to his own, and he knew that mammy looked upon him as an interloper.

Mima kept up well, only the paleness of her face showed what she felt at leaving her home. Her voice was calm and impassive, only once it trembled, when she wished that he would be as happy in the house as she had been.

"I feel very much like an interloper," he said, "but I hope you won't feel yourself entirely shut out from your beautiful home. My father, who comes on in a few days is an invalid, and gets about very little, and I am frequently from home, so pray make use of the grounds when you please, and as much of the house as you find convenient."

A cold "thank you" fell from Mima's lips, but then she went on, hesitatingly, "I should like to come sometimes to the hill, out there behind the orchard." Her voice choked, but she went bravely on, "Some of my dear ones are buried there."

"Go there, and elsewhere, as much as you please. That spot shall be sacred from invasion."

"You are very kind," she said and rose to go. Mammy carried away the tea things, and then came and waited silently by the door.

"I hope you will believe me, Miss Harrison," said Bartley, as Mima was starting, "when I say that I do not come to your home as a vandal to destroy all that makes its recollection dear to you; for there are some associations about it that are almost as much to me as to you, since my eyes have been opened."

"I do not understand you," she replied.

"I can explain. For some years past my father's condition has kept me very closely bound to him, and both before and after the beginning of the war, we lived abroad. A few years ago, I came to know and love a man, who I am convinced now was your brother. Am I mistaken in thinking that you are a sister of Philip Harrison?"

"No, no, he was my brother, my only brother."

"I met him in Venice just before the war and we came to be dear friends. But in the events that followed so tumultuously, and from participation in which, I was cut off by my father's illness, I lost sight of him."

"But I don't believe I remember hearing my brother speak of you, and he was not usually reticent."

"You would not remember me as Bartley Northcope, unless you were familiar with the very undignified sobriquet with which your brother nicknamed me," said the young man smiling.

"Nickname — what, you are not, you can't be 'Budge'?"

"I am 'Budge' or 'old Budge' as Phil called me."

Mima had her hand on the doorknob, but she turned with an impulsive motion and went back to him. "I am so glad to see you," she said, giving him her hand again, and "Mammy," she called, "Mr. Northcope is an old friend of brother Phil's!"

The effect of this news on mammy was like that of the April sun on an icicle. She suddenly melted, and came overflowing back into the room, her smiles and grins and nods trickling everywhere under the genial warmth of this new friendliness. Before one who had been a friend of "Mas' Phil's," Mammy Peggy needed no pride.

"La, chile," she exclaimed, settling and patting the cushions of the chair in which he had been sitting, "w'y didn' you say so befo'?"

"I wasn't sure that I was standing in the house of my old friend. I only knew that he lived somewhere in Virginia."

"He is among those out on the hill behind the orchard," said Mima, sadly. Mammy Peggy wiped her eyes, and went about trying to add some touches of comfort to the already perfect room.

"You have no reason to sorrow, Miss Harrison," said Northcope gently, "for a brother who died bravely in battle for his principles. Had fate allowed me to be here I should have been upon the other side, but believe me, I both understand and appreciate your brother's heroism."

The young girl's eyes glistened with tears, through which glowed her sisterly pride.

"Won't you come out and look at his grave?"

"It is the desire that was in my mind."

Together they walked out, with mammy following, to the old burying plot. All her talk was of her brother's virtues, and he proved an appreciative listener. She pointed out favorite spots of her brother's childhood as they passed along, and indicated others which his boyish pranks had made memorable, though the eyes of the man were oftener on her face than on the landscape. But it was with real sympathy and reverence that he stood with bared head beside the grave of his friend, and the tears that she left fall unchecked in his presence were not all tears of grief.

They did not go away from him that afternoon until Mammy Peggy, seconded by Mima, had won his consent to let the old servant come over and "do for him" until he found suitable servants.

"To think of his having known Philip," said Mima with shining eyes as they entered the new cottage, and somehow it looked pleasanter, brighter and less mean to her than it had ever before.

"Now s'posin' you'd 'a' run off widout seein' him, whaih would you been den? You wouldn' nevah knowed whut you knows."

"You're right, Mammy Peggy, and I'm glad I stayed and faced him, for it doesn't seem now as if a stranger had the house, and it has given me a great pleasure. It seemed like having Phil back again to have him talked about so by one who lived so near to him."

"I tell you, chile," mammy supplemented in an oracular tone, "de right kin' o' pride allus pays." Mima laughed heartily. The old woman looked at her bright face. Then she put her big hand on the girl's small one. It was trembling. She shook her head. Mima blushed.

Bartley went out and sat on the veranda a long time after they were gone. He took in the great expanse of lawn about the house, and the dark background of the pines in the woods beyond. He thought of the conditions through which the place had become his, and the thought saddened him, even in the first glow of the joy of possession. Then his mind went on to the old friend who was sleeping his last sleep back there on the sun-bathed hill. His recollection went fondly over the days of their comradeship in Venice, and colored them anew with glory.

"These Southerners," he mused aloud, "cannot understand that we sympathize with their misfortunes. But we do. They forget how our sympathies have been trained. We were first taught to sympathize with the slave, and now that he is free, and needs less, perhaps, of our sympathy, this, by a transition, as easy as it is natural, is transferred to his master. Poor, poor Phil!"

There was a strange emotion, half-sad, half-pleasant tugging at his heart. A mist came before his eyes and hid the landscape for a moment.

And he, he referred it all to the memories of the brother. Yes, he thought he was thinking of the brother, and he did not notice or did not pretend to notice that a pair of appealing eyes looking out beneath waves of brown hair, that a soft, fair hand, pressed in his own, floated nebulously at the back of his consciousness.

It was not until he had set out to furnish his house with a complement of servants against the coming of his father that Bartley came to realize the full worth of Mammy Peggy's offer to "do for him." The old woman not only got his meals and kept him comfortable, trudging over and back every day from the little cottage, but she proved invaluable in the choice of domestic help. She knew her people thereabouts, just who was spry, and who was trifling, and with the latter she would have nothing whatever to do. She acted rather as if he were a guest in his own house, and what was more would take no pay for it. Of course there had to be some return for so much kindness, and it took the form of various gifts of flowers and fruit from the old place to the new cottage. And sometimes when Bartley had forgotten to speak of it before mammy had left, he would arrange his baskets and carry his offering over himself. Mima thought it was very thoughtful and kind of him, and she wondered on these occasions if they ought not to keep Mr. Northcope to tea, and if mammy would not like to make some of those nice muffins of hers that he had liked so, and mammy always smiled on her charge, and said, "Yes, honey, yes, but hit do 'pear lak' dat Mistah No'thcope do fu'git mo' an' mo' to sen' de t'ings ovah by me w'en I's daih."

But mammy found her special charge when the elder Northcope came. It seemed that she could never do enough for the pale, stooped old man, and he declared that he had never felt better in his life than he grew to feel under her touch. An injury to his spine had resulted in partially disabling him, but his mind was a rich store of knowledge, and his disposition was tender and cheerful. So it pleased his son sometimes to bring Mima over to see him!

The warm, impulsive heart of the Southern girl went out to him, and they became friends at once. He found in her that soft, caressing, humoring quality that even his son's devotion could not supply, and his superior age, knowledge and wisdom made up to her the lost father's care for which Peggy's love illy substituted. The tenderness grew between them. Through the long afternoons she would read to him from his favorite books, or would listen to him as he talked of the lands where he had been, and the things he had seen. Sometimes Mammy Peggy grumbled at the reading, and said it "wuz jes' lak' doin' hiahed wo'k," but Mima only laughed and went on.

Bartley saw the sympathy between them and did not obtrude his presence, but often in the twilight when she started away, he would slip out of some corner and walk home with her.

These little walks together were very pleasant, and on one occasion he had asked her the question that made her pale and red by turns, and sent her heart beating with convulsive throbs that made her gasp.

"Maybe I'm over soon in asking you, Mima dear," he faltered, "but — but, I couldn't wait any longer. You've become a part of my life. I have no hope, no joy, no thought that you are not of. Won't you be my wife?"

They were pausing at her gate, and she was trembling from what emotion he only dared guess. But she did not answer. She only returned the pressure of his hand, and drawing it away, rushed into the house. She durst not trust her voice. Bartley went home walking on air.

Mima did not go directly to Mammy Peggy with her news. She must compose herself first. This was hard to do, so she went to her room and sat down to think it over.

"He loves me, he loves me," she kept saying to herself and with each repetition of the words, the red came anew into her cheeks. They were still a suspicious hue when she went into the kitchen to find mammy who was slumbering over the waiting dinner. "What meks you so long, honey," asked the old woman, coming wide awake out of her catnap.

"Oh, — I — I — I don't know," answered the young girl, blushing furiously, "I — I stopped to talk."

"Why dey ain no one in de house to talk to. I hyeahed you w'en you come home. You have been a powahful time sence you come in. Whut meks you so red?" Then a look of intelligence came into mammy's fat face, "Oomph," she said.

"Oh mammy, don't look that way, I couldn't help it. Bartley — Mr. Northcope has asked me to be his wife."

"Asked you to be his wife! Oomph! Whut did you tell him?"

"I didn't tell him anything. I was so ashamed I couldn't talk. I just ran away like a silly."

"Oomph," said mammy again, "an' whut you gwine to tell him?"

"Oh, I don't know. Don't you think he's a very nice young man, Mr. Northcope, mammy? And then his father's so nice."

Mammy's face clouded. "I doan' see whaih yo' Ha'ison pride is," she said; "co'se, he may be nice enough, but does you want to tell him yes de fust t'ing, so's he'll t'ink dat you jumped at de chanst to git him an' git back in de homestid?"

"Oh, mammy," cried Mima; she had gone all white and cold.

"You do' know nothin' 'bout his quality. You a Ha'ison yo'se'f. Who is he to be jumped at an' tuk at de fust axin'? Ef he wants you ve'y bad he'll ax mo' dan once."

"You needn't have reminded me, mammy, of who I am," said Mima. "I had no intention of telling Mr. Northcope yes. You needn't have been afraid for me." She fibbed a little, it is to be feared.

"Now don't talk dat 'way, chile. I know you laks him, an' I do' want to stop you f'om tekin' him. Don't you say no, ez ef you wasn' nevah gwine to say nothin' else. You jes' say a hol'in' off no."

"I like Mr. Northcope as a friend, and my no to him will be final."

The dinner did not go down very well with Mima that evening. It stopped in her throat, and when she swallowed, it brought the tears to her eyes. When it was done, she hurried away to her room.

She was so disappointed, but she would not confess it to herself, and she would not weep. "He proposed to me because he pitied me, oh, the shame of it! He turned me out of doors, and then thought I would be glad to come back at any price."

When he read her cold formal note, Bartley knew that he had offended her, and the thought burned him like fire. He cursed himself for a blundering fool. "She was only trying to be kind to father and me," he said, "and I have taken advantage of her goodness." He would never have confessed to himself before that he was a coward. But that morning when he got her note, he felt that he could not face her just yet, and commending his father to the tender mercies of Mammy Peggy and the servants, he took the first train to the north.

It would be hard to say which of the two was the most disappointed when the truth was known. It might better be said which of the three, for Mima went no more to the house, and the elder Northcope fretted and was restless without her. He availed himself of an invalid's privilege to be disagreeable, and nothing Mammy Peggy could do now would satisfy him. Indeed, between the two, the old woman had a hard time of it, for Mima was tearful and morose, and would not speak to her except to blame her. As the days went on she wished to all the powers that she had left the Harrison pride in the keeping of the direct members of the family. It had proven a dangerous thing in her hands.

Mammy soliloquized when she was about her work in the kitchen. "Men ain' whut dey used to be," she said, "who'd 'a' t'ought o' de young man a runnin' off dat away jes' 'cause a ooman tol' him no. He orter had sense enough to know dat a ooman has sev'al kin's o' noes. Now ef dat 'ud 'a' been in my day he'd a jes' stayed away to let huh t'ink hit ovah an' den come back an' axed huh ag'in. Den she could 'a' said yes all right an' proper widout a belittlin' huhse'f. But 'stead o' dat he mus' go a ta'in' off jes' ez soon ez de fus' wo'ds come outen huh mouf. Put' nigh brekin' huh hea't. I clah to goodness, I nevah did see sich ca'in's on."

Several weeks passed before Bartley returned to his home. Autumn was painting the trees about the place before the necessity of being at his father's side called him from his voluntary exile. And then he did not go to see Mima. He was still bowed with shame at what he thought his unmanly presumption, and he did not blame her that she avoided him.

His attention was arrested one day about a week after his return by the peculiar actions of Mammy Peggy. She hung around him, and watched him, following him from place to place like a spaniel.

Finally he broke into a laugh and said, "Why, what's the matter, Aunt Peggy, are you afraid I'm going to run away?"

"No, I ain' afeared o' dat," said mammy, meekly, "but I been had somepn' to say to you dis long w'ile."

"Well, go ahead, I'm listening."

Mammy gulped and went on. "Ask huh ag'in," she said, "it were my fault she tol' you no. I 'minded huh o' huh fambly pride an' tol' huh to hol' you off less'n you'd t'ink she wan'ed to jump at you."

Bartley was on his feet in a minute.

"What does this mean," he cried. "Is it true, didn't I offend her?"

"No, you didn' 'fend huh. She's been pinin' fu' you, 'twell she's growed right peekid."

"Sh, auntie, do you mean to tell me that Mim — Miss Harrison cares for me?"

"You go an' ax huh ag'in."

Bartley needed no second invitation. He flew to the cottage. Mima's heart gave a great throb when she saw him coming up the walk, and she tried to harden herself against him. But her lips would twitch, and her voice would tremble as she said, "How do you do, Mr. Northcope?"

He looked keenly into her eyes.

"Have I been mistaken, Mima," he said, "in believing that I greatly offended you by asking you to be my wife? Do you — can you care for me, darling?"

The words stuck in her throat, and he went on, "I thought you were angry with me because I had taken advantage of your kindness to my father, or presumed upon any kindness that you may have felt for me out of respect to your brother's memory. Believe me, I was innocent of any such intention."

"Oh, it wasn't — it wasn't that!" she gasped.

"Then won't you give me a different answer," he said, taking her hand.

"I can't, I can't," she cried.

"Why, Mima?" he asked.

"Because —"

"Because of the Harrison pride?"

"Bartley!"

"Your Mammy Peggy has confessed all to me."

"Mammy Peggy!"

"Yes."

She tried hard to stiffen herself. "Then it is all out of the question," she began.

"Don't let any little folly or pride stand between us," he broke in, drawing her to him.

She gave up the struggle, and her head dropped upon his shoulder for a moment. Then she lifted her eyes, shining with tears to his face, and said, "Bartley, it wasn't my pride, it was Mammy Peggy's."

He cut off further remarks.

When he was gone, and mammy came in after a while, Mima ran to her crying,

"Oh, mammy, mammy, you bad, stupid, dear old goose!" and she buried her head in the old woman's lap.

"Oomph," grunted mammy, "I said de right kin' o' pride allus pays. But de wrong kin' — oomph, well, you'd bettah look out!"

VINEY'S FREE PAPERS

PART I

There was joy in the bosom of Ben Raymond. He sang as he hoed in the field. He cheerfully worked overtime and his labors did not make him tired. When the quitting horn blew he executed a double shuffle as he shouldered his hoe and started for his cabin. While the other men dragged wearily over the ground he sprang along as if all day long he had not been bending over the hoe in the hot sun, with the sweat streaming from his face in rivulets.

And this had been going on for two months now — two happy months — ever since Viney had laid her hand in his, had answered with a coquettish "Yes," and the master had given his consent, his blessing and a five-dollar bill.

It had been a long and trying courtship — that is, it had been trying for Ben, because Viney loved pleasure and hungered for attention and the field was full of rivals. She was a merry girl and a pretty one. No one could dance better; no girl on the place was better able to dress her dark charms to advantage or to show them off more temptingly. The toss of her head was an invitation and a challenge in one, and the way she smiled back at them over her shoulder, set the young men's heads dancing and their hearts throbbing. So her suitors were many. But through it all Ben was patient, unflinching and faithful, and finally, after leading him a life full of doubt and suspense, the coquette surrendered and gave herself into his keeping.

She was maid to her mistress, but she had time, nevertheless, to take care of the newly whitewashed cabin in the quarters to which Ben took her. And it was very pleasant to lean over and watch him at work making things for the little house — a chair from a barrel and a wonderful box of shelves to stand in the corner. And she knew how to say merry things, and later outside his door Ben would pick his banjo and sing low and sweetly in the musical voice of his race. Altogether such another honeymoon there had never been.

For once the old women hushed up their prophecies of evil, although in the beginning they had shaken their wise old turbaned heads and predicted that marriage with such a flighty creature as Viney could come to no good. They had said among themselves that Ben would better marry some good, solid-minded, strong-armed girl who would think more about work than about pleasures and coquetting.

"I 'low, honey," an old woman had said, "she'll mek his heart ache many a time. She'll comb his haid wid a three-legged stool an' bresh it wid de broom. Uh, huh — putty, is she? You ma'y huh 'cause she putty. Ki-yi! She fix you! Putty women fu' putty tricks."

And the old hag smacked her lips over the spice of malevolence in her words. Some women — and they are not all black and ugly — never forgive the world for letting them grow old.

But, in spite of all prophecies to the contrary, two months of unalloyed joy had passed for Ben and Viney, and tonight the climax seemed to have been reached. Ben hurried along, talking to himself as his hoe swung over his shoulder.

"Kin I do it?" he was saying. "Kin I do it?" Then he would stop his walk and his cogitations would bloom into a mirthful chuckle. Something very pleasant was passing through his mind.

As he approached, Viney was standing in the door of the little cabin, whose white sides with green Madeira clambering over them made a pretty frame for the dark girl in her print dress. The husband bent double at sight of her, stopped, took off his hat, slapped his knee, and relieved his feelings by a sounding "Who-ee!"

"What's de mattah wid you, Ben? You ac' lak you mighty happy. Bettah come on in hyeah an' git yo' suppah fo' hit gits col'."

For answer, the big fellow dropped the hoe and, seizing the slight form in his arms, swung her around until she gasped for breath.

"Oh, Ben," she shrieked, "you done tuk all my win'!"

"Dah, now," he said, letting her down; "dat's what you gits fu' talkin' sassy to me!"

"Nev' min'; I'm goin' to fix you fu' dat fus' time I gits de chanst — see ef I don't."

"Whut you gwine do? Gwine to pizen me?"

"Worse'n dat!"

"Wuss'n dat? Whut you gwine fin' any wuss'n pizenin' me, less'n you conjuh me?"

"Huh uh — still worse'n dat. I'm goin' to leave you."

"Huh uh — no you ain', 'cause any place you'd go you wouldn' no more'n git dah twell you'd tu'n erroun' all of er sudden an' say, 'Why, dah's Ben!' an' dah I'd be."

They chattered on like children while she was putting the supper on the table and he was laving his hot face in the basin beside the door.

"I got great news fu' you," he said, as they sat down.

"I bet you ain' got nothin' of de kin'."

"All right. Den dey ain' no use in me a tryin' to 'vince you. I jes' be wastin' my bref."

"Go on — tell me, Ben."

"Huh uh — you bet you ain', an' ef I tell you you lose de bet."

"I don' keer. Ef you don' tell me, den I know you ain' got no news worth tellin'.'"

"Ain' go no news wuff tellin'! Who-ee!"

He came near choking on a gulp of coffee, and again his knee suffered from the pounding of his great hands.

"Huccume you so full of laugh tonight?" she asked, laughing with him.

"How you 'spec' I gwine tell you dat less'n I tell you my sec'ut?"

"Well, den, go on — tell me yo' sec'ut."

"Huh uh. You done bet it ain' wuff tellin'."

"I don't keer what I bet. I wan' to hyeah it now. Please, Ben, please!"

"Listen how she baig! Well, I gwine tell you now. I ain' gwine tease you no mo'."

She bent her head forward expectantly.

"I had a talk wid Mas' Raymond today," resumed Ben.

"Yes?"

"An' he say he pay me all my back money fu' ovahtime."

"Oh!"

"An' all I gits right along he gwine he'p me save, an' when I git fo' hund'ed dollahs he gwine gin me de free papahs fu' you, my little gal."

"Oh, Ben, Ben! Hit ain' so, is it?"

"Yes, hit is. Den you'll be you own ooman — leas'ways less'n you wants to be mine."

She went and put her arms around his neck. Her eyes were sparkling and her lips quivering.

"You don' mean, Ben, dat I'll be free?"

"Yes, you'll be free, Viney. Den I's gwine to set to wo'k an' buy my free papahs."

"Oh, kin you do it — kin you do it — kin you do it?"

"Kin I do it?" he repeated. He stretched out his arm, with the sleeve rolled to the shoulder, and curved it upward till the muscles stood out like great knots of oak. Then he opened and shut his fingers, squeezing them together until the joints cracked. "Kin I do it?" He looked down on her calmly and smiled simply, happily.

She threw her arms around his waist and sank on her knees at his feet sobbing.

"Ben, Ben! My Ben! I nevah even thought of it. Hit seemed so far away, but now we're goin' to be free — free, free!"

He lifted her up gently.

"It's gwine to tek a pow'ful long time," he said.

"I don' keer," she cried gaily. "We know it's comin' an' we kin wait."

The woman's serious mood had passed as quickly as it had come, and she spun around the cabin, executing a series of steps that set her husband a-grin with admiration and joy.

And so Ben began to work with renewed vigor. He had found a purpose in life and there was something for him to look for beyond dinner, a dance and the end of the day. He had always been a good hand, but now he became a model — no shirking, no shiftlessness — and because he was so earnest his master did what he could to help him. Numerous little plans were formulated whereby the slave could make or save a precious dollar.

Viney, too, seemed inspired by a new hope, and if this little house had been pleasant to Ben, nothing now was wanting to make it a palace in his eyes. Only one sorrow he had, and that one wrung hard at his great heart — no baby came to them — but instead he made a great baby of his wife, and went on his way hiding his disappointment the best he could. The banjo was often silent now, for when he came home his fingers were too stiff to play; but sometimes, when his heart ached for the laughter of a child, he would take down his old friend and play low, soothing melodies until he found rest and comfort.

Viney had once tried to console him by saying that had she had a child it would have taken her away from her work, but he had only answered, "We could a' stood that."

But Ben's patient work and frugality had their reward, and it was only a little over three years after he had set out to do it that he put in his master's hand the price of Viney's freedom, and there was sound of rejoicing in the land. A fat shoat, honestly come by — for it was the master's gift — was killed and baked, great jugs of biting persimmon beer were brought forth, and the quarters held high carnival to celebrate Viney's new-found liberty.

After the merrymakers had gone, and when the cabin was clear again, Ben held out the paper that had been on exhibition all evening to Viney.

"Hyeah, hyeah's de docyment dat meks you yo' own ooman. Tek it."

During all the time that it had been out for show that night the people had looked upon it with a sort of awe, as if it was possessed of some sort of miraculous power. Even now Viney did not take hold of it, but shrunk away with a sort of gasp.

"No, Ben, you keep it. I can't tek keer o' no sich precious thing ez dat. Put hit in yo' chist."

"Tek hit and feel of hit, anyhow, so's you'll know dat you's free."

She took it gingerly between her thumb and forefinger. Ben suddenly let go.

"Dah, now," he said; "you keep dat docment. It's yo's. Keep hit undah yo' own 'sponsibility."

"No, no, Ben!" she cried. "I jes' can't!"

"You mus'. Dat's de way to git used to bein' free. Whenevah you looks at yo'se'f an' feels lak you ain' no diff'ent f'om whut you been you tek dat papah out an' look at hit, an' say to yo'se'f, 'Dat means freedom.'"

Carefully, reverently, silently Viney put the paper into her bosom.

"Now, de nex' t'ing fu' me to do is to set out to git one dem papahs fu' myse'f. Hit'll be a long try, 'cause I can't buy mine so cheap as I got yo's, dough de Lawd knows why a great big ol' hunk lak me should cos' mo'n a precious mossell lak you."

"Hit's because dey's so much of you, Ben, an' evah bit of you's wo'th its weight in gol'."

"Heish, chile! Don' put my valy so high, er I'll be twell jedgment day a-payin' hit off."

PART II

So Ben went forth to battle for his own freedom, undaunted by the task before him, while Viney took care of the cabin, doing what she could outside. Armed with her new dignity, she insisted upon her friends' recognizing the change in her condition.

Thus, when Mandy so far forgot herself as to address her as Viney Raymond, the new free woman's head went up and she said with withering emphasis:

"Mis' Viney Allen, if you please!"

"Viney Allen!" exclaimed her visitor. "Huccum you's Viney Allen now?"

"'Cause I don' belong to de Raymonds no mo', an' I kin tek my own name now."

"Ben 'longs to de Raymonds, an' his name Ben Raymond an' you his wife. How you git aroun' dat, Mis' Viney Allen?"

"Ben's name goin' to be Mistah Allen soon's he gits his free papahs."

"Oomph! You done gone now! Yo' naik so stiff you can't ha'dly ben' it. I don' see how dat papah mek sich a change in anybody's actions. Yo' face ain' got no whitah."

"No, but I's free, an' I kin do as I please."

Mandy went forth and spread the news that Viney had changed her name from Raymond to Allen. "She's Mis' Viney Allen, if you please!" was her comment. Great was the indignation among the older heads whose fathers and mothers and grandfathers before them had been Raymonds. The younger element was greatly amused and took no end of pleasure in repeating the new name or addressing each other by fantastic cognomens. Viney's popularity did not increase.

Some rumors of this state of things drifted to Ben's ears and he questioned his wife about them. She admitted what she had done.

"But, Viney," said Ben, "Raymond's good enough name fu' me."

"Don' you see, Ben," she answered, "dat I don' belong to de Raymonds no mo', so I ain' Viney Raymond. Ain' you goin' change w'en you git free?"

"I don' know. I talk about dat when I's free, and freedom's a mighty long, weary way off yet."

"Evahbody dat's free has dey own name, an' I ain' nevah goin' feel free's long ez I's a-totin' aroun' de Raymonds' name."

"Well, change den," said Ben; "but wait ontwell I kin change wid you."

Viney tossed her head, and that night she took out her free papers and studied them long and carefully.

She was incensed at her friends that they would not pay her the homage that she felt was due her. She was incensed at Ben because he would not enter into her feelings about the matter. She brooded upon her fancied injuries, and when a chance for revenge came she seized upon it eagerly.

There were two or three free negro families in the vicinity of the Raymond place, but there had been no intercourse between them and the neighboring slaves. It was to these people that Viney now turned in anger against her own friends. It first amounted to a few visits back and forth, and then, either because the association became more intimate or because she was instigated to it by her new companions, she refused to have anything more to do with the Raymond servants. Boldly and without concealment she shut the door in Mandy's face, and, hearing this, few of the others gave her a similar chance.

Ben remonstrated with her, and she answered him:

"No, suh! I ain' goin' 'sociate wid slaves! I's free!"

"But you cuttin' out yo' own husban'."

"Dat's diff'ent. I's jined to my husban'." And then petulantly: "I do wish you'd hu'y up an' git yo' free papahs, Ben."

"Dey'll be a long time a-comin'," he said; "yeahs f'om now. Mebbe I'd abettah got mine fust."

She looked up at him with a quick, suspicious glance. When she was alone again she took her papers and carefully hid them.

"I's free," she whispered to herself, "an' I don' expec' to nevah be a slave no mo'."

She was further excited by the moving North of one of the free families with which she had been associated. The emigrants had painted glowing pictures of the Eldorado to which they were going, and now Viney's only talk in the evening was of the glories of the North. Ben would listen to her unmoved, until one night she said:

"You ought to go North when you gits yo' papahs."

Then he had answered her, with kindling eyes:

"No, I won't go Nawth! I was bo'n an' raised in de Souf, an' in de Souf I stay ontwell I die. Ef I have to go Nawth to injoy my freedom I won't have it. I'll quit wo'kin fu' it."

Ben was positive, but he felt uneasy, and the next day he told his master of the whole matter, and Mr. Raymond went down to talk to Viney.

She met him with a determination that surprised and angered him. To everything he said to her she made but one answer: "I's got my free papahs an' I's a-goin' Nawth."

Finally her former master left her with the remark:

"Well, I don't care where you go, but I'm sorry for Ben. He was a fool for working for you. You don't half deserve such a man."

"I won' have him long," she flung after him, with a laugh.

The opposition with which she had met seemed to have made her more obstinate, and in spite of all Ben could do, she began to make preparations to leave him. The money for the chickens and eggs had been growing and was to have gone toward her husband's ransom, but she finally sold all her laying hens to increase the amount. Then she calmly announced to her husband:

"I's got money enough an' I's a-goin' Nawth next week. You kin stay down hyeah an' be a slave ef you want to, but I's a-goin' Nawth."

"Even ef I wanted to go Nawth you know I ain' half paid out yit."

"Well, I can't he'p it. I can't spen' all de bes' pa't o' my life down hyeah where dey ain' no 'vantages."

"I reckon dey's 'vantages everywhah fu' anybody dat wants to wu'k."

"Yes, but what kin o' wages does yo' git? Why, de Johnsons say dey had a lettah f'om Miss Smiff an' dey's gettin' 'long fine in de Nawth."

"De Johnsons ain' gwine?"

"Si Johnson is —"

Then the woman stopped suddenly.

"Oh, hit's Si Johnson? Huh!"

"He ain' goin' wid me. He's jes' goin' to see dat I git sta'ted right aftah I git thaih."

"Hit's Si Johnson?" he repeated.

"'Tain't," said the woman. "Hit's freedom."

Ben got up and went out of the cabin.

"Men's so 'spicious," she said. "I ain' goin' Nawth 'cause Si's a-goin' — I ain't."

When Mr. Raymond found out how matters were really going he went to Ben where he was at work in the field.

"Now, look here, Ben," he said. "You're one of the best hands on my place and I'd be sorry to lose you. I never did believe in this buying business from the first, but you were so bent on it that I gave in. But before I'll see her cheat you out of your money I'll give you your free papers now. You can go North with her and you can pay me back when you find work."

"No," replied Ben doggedly. "Ef she cain't wait fu' me she don' want me, an' I won't roller her erroun' an' be in de way."

"You're a fool!" said his master.

"I loves huh," said the slave. And so this plan came to naught.

Then came the night on which Viney was getting together her belongings. Ben sat in a corner of the cabin silent, his head bowed in his hands. Every once in a while the woman cast a half-frightened glance at him. He had never once tried to oppose her with force, though she saw that grief had worn lines into his face.

The door opened and Si Johnson came in. He had just dropped in to see if everything was all right. He was not to go for a week.

"Let me look at yo' free papahs," he said, for Si could read and liked to show off his accomplishment at every opportunity. He stumbled through the formal document to the end, reading at the last: "This is a present from Ben to his beloved wife, Viney."

She held out her hand for the paper. When Si was gone she sat gazing at it, trying in her ignorance to pick from the, to her, senseless scrawl those last words. Ben had not raised his head.

Still she sat there, thinking, and without looking her mind began to take in the details of the cabin. That box of shelves there in the corner Ben had made in the first days they were together. Yes, and this chair on which she was sitting — she remembered how they had laughed over its funny shape before he had padded it with cotton and covered it with the piece of linsey "old Mis'" had given him. The very chest in which her things were packed he had made, and when the last nail was driven he had called it her trunk, and said she should put her finery in it when she went traveling like the white folks. She was going traveling now, and Ben — Ben? There he sat across from her in his chair, bowed and broken, his great shoulders heaving with suppressed grief.

Then, before she knew it, Viney was sobbing, and had crept close to him and put her arms around his neck. He threw out his arms with a convulsive gesture and gathered her up to his breast, and the tears gushed from his eyes.

When the first storm of weeping had passed Viney rose and went to the fireplace. She raked forward the coals.

"Ben," she said, "hit's been dese pleggoned free papahs. I want you to see em bu'n."

"No, no!" he said. But the papers were already curling, and in a moment they were in a blaze.

"Thaih," she said, "thaih, now, Viney Raymond!"

Ben gave a great gasp, then sprang forward and took her in his arms and kicked the packed chest into the corner.

And that night singing was heard from Ben's cabin and the sound of the banjo.

THE FRUITFUL SLEEPING OF
THE REV. ELISHA EDWARDS

There was great commotion in Zion Church, a body of Christian wor-shippers, usually noted for their harmony. But for the last six months, trouble had been brewing between the congregation and the pastor. The Rev. Elisha Edwards had come to them two years before, and he had given good satisfaction as to preaching and pastoral work. Only one thing had dis-pleased his congregation in him, and that was his tendency to moments of meditative abstraction in the pulpit. However much fire he might have dis-played before a brother minister arose to speak, and however much he might display in the exhortation after the brother was done with the labors of hurling phillipics against the devil, he sat between in the same way, with head bowed and eyes closed.

There were some who held that it was a sign in him of deep thoughtful-ness, and that he was using these moments for silent prayer and meditation. But others, less generous, said that he was either jealous of or indifferent to other speakers. So the discussion rolled on about the Rev. Elisha, but it did not reach him and he went on in the same way until one hapless day, one tragic, one never-to-be-forgotten day. While Uncle Isham Dyer was exhorting the people to repent of their sins, the disclosure came. The old man had arisen on the wings of his eloquence and was painting hell for the sinners in the most terrible colors, when to the utter surprise of the whole congrega-tion, a loud and penetrating snore broke from the throat of the pastor of the church. It rumbled down the silence and startled the congregation into sudden and indignant life like the surprising cannon of an invading host. Horror-stricken eyes looked into each other, hands were thrown into the air, and heavy lips made round O's of surprise and anger. This was his medita-tion. The Rev. Elisha Edwards was asleep!

Uncle Isham Dyer turned around and looked down on his pastor in dis-gust, and then turned again to his exhortations, but he was disconcerted, and soon ended lamely.

As for the Rev. Elisha himself, his snore rumbled on through the church, his head drooped lower, until with a jerk, he awakened himself. He sighed religiously, patted his foot upon the floor, rubbed his hands together, and looked complacently over the aggrieved congregation. Old ladies moaned and old men shivered, but the pastor did not know what they had discovered, and shouted Amen, because he thought something Uncle Isham had said was affecting them. Then, when he arose to put the cap sheaf on his local brother's exhortations, he was strong, fiery, eloquent, but it was of no use. Not a cry, not a moan, not an Amen could he gain from his congregation. Only the local preacher himself, thinking over the scene which had just been enacted, raised his voice, placed his hands before his eyes, and murmured, "Lord he'p we po' sinnahs!"

Brother Edwards could not understand this unresponsiveness on the part of his people. They had been wont to weave and moan and shout and sigh when he spoke to them, and when, in the midst of his sermon, he paused to break into spirited song, they would join with him until the church rang again. But this day, he sang alone, and ominous glances were flashed from pew to pew and from aisle to pulpit. The collection that morning was especially small. No one asked the minister home to dinner, an unusual thing, and so he went his way, puzzled and wondering.

Before church that night, the congregation met together for conference. The exhorter of the morning himself opened proceedings by saying, "Brothahs an' sistahs, de Lawd has opened ouah eyes to wickedness in high places."

"Oom — oom — oom, he have opened ouah eyes," moaned an old sister.

"We have been puhmitted to see de man who was intrusted wid de guidance of dis flock a-sleepin' in de houah of duty, an' we feels grieved ternight."

"He sholy were asleep," sister Hannah Johnson broke in, "dey ain't no way to 'spute dat, dat man sholy were asleep."

"I kin testify to it," said another sister, "I p'intly did hyeah him sno', an' I hyeahed him sno't w'en he waked up."

"An' we been givin' him praise fu' meditation," pursued Brother Isham Dyer, who was only a local preacher, in fact, but who had designs on ordination, and the pastoring of Zion Church himself.

"It ain't de sleepin' itse'f," he went on, "ef you 'member in de Gyarden of Gethsemane, endurin' de agony of ouah Lawd, dem what he tuk wid him fu' to watch while he prayed, went to sleep on his han's. But he fu'give 'em, fu' he said, 'De sperit is willin' but de flesh is weak.' We know dat dey is times w'en de eyes grow sandy, an' de haid grow heavy, an' we ain't accusin' ouah brothah, nor a-blamin' him fu' noddin'. But what we do blame him fu' is fu' 'ceivin' us, an' mekin' us believe he was prayin' an' meditatin', w'en he wasn' doin' a blessed thing but snoozin'."

"Dat's it, dat's it," broke in a chorus of voices. "He 'ceived us, dat's what he did."

The meeting went stormily on, the accusation and the anger of the people against the minister growing more and more. One or two were for dismissing him then and there, but calmer counsel prevailed and it was decided to give him another trial. He was a good preacher they had to admit. He had visited them when they were sick, and brought sympathy to their afflictions, and a genial presence when they were well. They would not throw him over, without one more chance, at least, of vindicating himself.

This was well for the Rev. Elisha, for with the knowledge that he was to be given another chance, one trembling little woman, who had listened in silence and fear to the tirades against him, crept out of the church, and hastened over in the direction of the parsonage. She met the preacher coming toward the church, hymn-book in hand, and his Bible under his arm. With a gasp, she caught him by the arm, and turned him back.

"Come hyeah," she said, "come hyeah, dey been talkin' 'bout you, an' I want to tell you."

"Why, Sis' Dicey," said the minister complacently, "what is the mattah? Is you troubled in sperit?"

"I's troubled in sperit now," she answered, "but you'll be troubled in a minute. Dey done had a church meetin' befo' services. Dey foun' out you was sleepin' dis mornin' in de pulpit. You ain't only sno'ed, but you sno'ted, an' dey 'lowin' to give you one mo' trial, an' ef you falls f'om grace agin, dey gwine ax you fu' to 'sign f'om de pastorship."

The minister staggered under the blow, and his brow wrinkled. To leave Zion Church. It would be very hard. And to leave there in disgrace; where would he go? His career would be ruined. The story would go to every church of the connection in the country, and he would be an outcast from his cloth and his kind. He felt that it was all a mistake after all. He loved his work, and he loved his people. He wanted to do the right thing, but oh, sometimes, the chapel was hot and the hours were long. Then his head would grow heavy, and his eyes would close, but it had been only for a minute or two. Then, this morning, he remembered how he had tried to shake himself awake, how gradually, the feeling had overcome him. Then — then — he had snored. He had not tried wantonly to deceive them, but the Book said, "Let not thy right hand know what thy left hand doeth." He did not think it necessary to tell them that he dropped into an occasional nap in church. Now, however, they knew all.

He turned and looked down at the little woman, who waited to hear what he had to say.

"Thankye, ma'am, Sis' Dicey," he said. "Thankye, ma'am. I believe I'll go back an' pray ovah this subject." And he turned and went back into the parsonage.

Whether he had prayed over it or whether he had merely thought over it, and made his plans accordingly, when the Rev. Elisha came into church that night, he walked with a new spirit. There was a smile on his lips, and the light of triumph in his eyes. Throughout the Deacon's long prayer, his loud and insistent Amens precluded the possibility of any sleep on his part. His sermon was a masterpiece of fiery eloquence, and as Sister Green stepped out of the church door that night, she said, "Well, ef Brothah Eddards slep' dis mornin', he sholy prached a wakenin' up sermon ternight." The congregation hardly remembered that their pastor had ever been asleep. But the pastor knew when the first flush of enthusiasm was over that their minds would revert to the crime of the morning, and he made plans accordingly for the next Sunday which should again vindicate him in the eyes of his congregation.

The Sunday came round, and as he ascended to the pulpit, their eyes were fastened upon him with suspicious glances. Uncle Isham Dyer had a smile of triumph on his face, because the day was a particularly hot and drowsy one. It was on this account, the old man thought, that the Rev. Elisha asked him to say a few words at the opening of the meeting. "Shirkin' again," said the old man to himself, "I reckon he wants to go to sleep again, but ef he don't sleep dis day to his own confusion, I ain't hyeah." So he arose, and burst into a wonderful exhortation on the merits of a Christian life.

He had scarcely been talking for five minutes, when the ever watchful congregation saw the pastor's head droop, and his eyes close. For the next fifteen minutes, little or no attention was paid to Brother Dyer's exhortation. The angry people were nudging each other, whispering, and casting indignant glances at the sleeping pastor. He awoke and sat up, just as the exhorter was finishing in a fiery period. If those who watched him, were expecting to see any embarrassed look on his face, or show of timidity in his eyes, they were mistaken. Instead, his appearance was one of sudden alertness, and his gaze that of a man in extreme exaltation. One would have said that it had been given to him as to the inspired prophets of old to see and to hear things far and beyond the ken of ordinary mortals. As Brother Dyer sat down, he arose quickly and went forward to the front of the pulpit with a firm step. Still, with the look of exaltation on his face, he announced his text, "Ef he sleep he shell do well."

The congregation, which a moment before had been all indignation, suddenly sprang into the most alert attention. There was a visible pricking up of ears as the preacher entered into his subject. He spoke first of the benefits of sleep, what it did for the worn human body and the weary human soul, then turning off into a half-humorous, half-quizzical strain, which was often in his sermons, he spoke of how many times he had to forgive some of those who sat before him today for nodding in their pews; then raising his voice, like a good preacher, he came back to his text, exclaiming, "But ef he sleep, he shell do well."

He went on then, and told of Jacob's sleep, and how at night, in the midst of his slumbers the visions of angels had come to him, and he had left a testimony behind him that was still a solace to their hearts. Then he lowered his voice and said:

"You all condemns a man when you sees him asleep, not knowin' what visions is a-goin' thoo his mind, nor what feelin's is a-goin thoo his heart. You ain't conside'in' that mebbe he's a-doin' mo' in the soul wo'k when he's asleep then when he's awake. Mebbe he sleep, w'en you think he ought to be up a-wo'kin'. Mebbe he slumber w'en you think he ought to be up an' erbout. Mebbe he sno' an' mebbe he sno't, but I'm a-hyeah to tell you, in de wo'ds of the Book, that they ain't no 'sputin' 'Ef he sleep, he shell do well!'"

"Yes, Lawd!" "Amen!" "Sleep on Ed'ards!" some one shouted. The church was in smiles of joy. They were rocking to and fro with the ecstasy of the sermon, but the Rev. Elisha had not yet put on the cap sheaf.

"Hol' on," he said, "befo' you shouts er befo' you sanctions. Fu' you may yet have to tu'n yo' backs erpon me, an' say, 'Lawd he'p the man!' I's a-hyeah to tell you that many's the time in this very pulpit, right under yo' very eyes, I has gone f'om meditation into slumber. But what was the reason? Was I a-shirkin' er was I lazy?"

Shouts of "No! No!" from the congregation.

"No, no," pursued the preacher, "I wasn't a-shirkin' ner I wasn't a-lazy, but the soul within me was a wo'kin' wid the min', an' as we all gwine ter do some day befo' long, early in de mornin', I done fu'git this ol' body. My haid fall on my breas', my eyes close, an' I see visions of anothah day to come. I see visions of a new Heaven an' a new earth, when we shell all be clothed in white raimen', an' we shell play ha'ps of gol', an' walk de golden streets of the New Jerusalem! That's what been a runnin' thoo my min', w'en I set up in the pulpit an' sleep under the Wo'd; but I want to ax you, was I wrong? I want to ax you, was I sinnin'? I want to p'int you right hyeah to the Wo'd, as it are read out in yo' hyeahin' terday, 'Ef he sleep, he shell do well.'"

The Rev. Elisha ended his sermon amid the smiles and nods and tears of his congregation. No one had a harsh word for him now, and even Brother Dyer wiped his eyes and whispered to his next neighbor, "Dat man sholy did sleep to some pu'pose," although he knew that the dictum was a deathblow to his own pastoral hopes. The people thronged around the pastor as he descended from the pulpit, and held his hand as they had done of yore. One old woman went out, still mumbling under her breath, "Sleep on, Ed'ards, sleep on."

There were no more church meetings after that, and no tendency to dismiss the pastor. On the contrary, they gave him a donation party next week, at which Sister Dicey helped him to receive his guests.

THE INGRATE

I

Mr. Leckler was a man of high principle. Indeed, he himself had admitted it at times to Mrs. Leckler. She was often called into counsel with him. He was one of those large souled creatures with a hunger for unlimited advice, upon which he never acted. Mrs. Leckler knew this, but like the good, patient little wife that she was, she went on paying her poor tribute of advice and admiration. To-day her husband's mind was particularly troubled, — as usual, too, over a matter of principle. Mrs. Leckler came at his call.

"Mrs. Leckler," he said, "I am troubled in my mind. I — in fact, I am puzzled over a matter that involves either the maintaining or relinquishing of a principle."

"Well, Mr. Leckler?" said his wife, interrogatively.

"If I had been a scheming, calculating Yankee, I should have been rich now; but all my life I have been too generous and confiding. I have always let principle stand between me and my interests." Mr. Leckler took himself all too seriously to be conscious of his pun, and went on: "Now this is a matter in which my duty and my principles seem to conflict. It stands thus: Josh has been doing a piece of plastering for Mr. Eckley over in Lexington, and from what he says, I think that city rascal has misrepresented the amount of work to me and so cut down the pay for it. Now, of course, I should not care, the matter of a dollar or two being nothing to me; but it is a very different matter when we consider poor Josh." There was deep pathos in Mr. Leckler's tone. "You know Josh is anxious to buy his freedom, and I allow him a part of whatever he makes; so you see it's he that's affected. Every dollar that he is cheated out of cuts off just so much from his earnings, and puts further away his hope of emancipation."

If the thought occurred to Mrs. Leckler that, since Josh received only about one-tenth of what he earned, the advantage of just wages would be quite as much her husband's as the slave's, she did not betray it, but met the naïve reasoning with the question, "But where does the conflict come in, Mr. Leckler?"

"Just here. If Josh knew how to read and write and cipher —"

"Mr. Leckler, are you crazy!"

"Listen to me, my dear, and give me the benefit of your judgment. This is a very momentous question. As I was about to say, if Josh knew these things, he could protect himself from cheating when his work is at too great a distance for me to look after it for him."

"But teaching a slave —"

"Yes, that's just what is against my principles. I know how public opinion and the law look at it. But my conscience rises up in rebellion every time I think of that poor black man being cheated out of his earnings. Really, Mrs. Leckler, I think I may trust to Josh's discretion, and secretly give him such instructions as will permit him to protect himself."

"Well, of course, it's just as you think best," said his wife.

"I knew you would agree with me," he returned. "It's such a comfort to take counsel with you, my dear!" And the generous man walked out on to the veranda, very well satisfied with himself and his wife, and prospectively pleased with Josh. Once he murmured to himself, "I'll lay for Eckley next time."

Josh, the subject of Mr. Leckler's charitable solicitations, was the plantation plasterer. His master had given him his trade, in order that he might do whatever such work was needed about the place; but he became so proficient in his duties, having also no competition among the poor whites, that he had grown to be in great demand in the country thereabout. So Mr. Leckler found it profitable, instead of letting him do chores and field work in his idle time, to hire him out to neighboring farms and planters. Josh was a man of more than ordinary intelligence; and when he asked to be allowed to pay for himself by working overtime, his master readily agreed, — for it promised more work to be done, for which he could allow the slave just what he pleased. Of course, he knew now that when the black man began to cipher this state of affairs would be changed; but it would mean such an increase of profit from the outside, that he could afford to give up his own little peculations. Anyway, it would be many years before the slave could pay the two thousand dollars, which price he had set upon him. Should he approach that figure, Mr. Leckler felt it just possible that the market in slaves would take a sudden rise.

When Josh was told of his master's intention, his eyes gleamed with pleasure, and he went to his work with the zest of long hunger. He proved a remarkably apt pupil. He was indefatigable in doing the tasks assigned him. Even Mr. Leckler, who had great faith in his plasterer's ability, marveled at the speed which he had acquired the three R's. He did not know that on one of his many trips a free negro had given Josh the rudimentary tools of learning, and that since the slave had been adding to his store of learning by poring over signs and every bit of print that he could spell out. Neither was Josh so indiscreet as to intimate to his benefactor that he had been anticipated in his good intentions.

It was in this way, working and learning, that a year passed away, and Mr. Leckler thought that his object had been accomplished. He could safely trust Josh to protect his own interests, and so he thought that it was quite time that his servant's education should cease.

"You know, Josh," he said, "I have already gone against my principles and against the law for your sake, and of course a man can't stretch his conscience too far, even to help another who's being cheated; but I reckon you can take care of yourself now."

"Oh, yes, suh, I reckon I kin," said Josh.

"And it wouldn't do for you to be seen with any books about you now."

"Oh, no, suh, su't'n'y not." He didn't intend to be seen with any books about him.

It was just now that Mr. Leckler saw the good results of all he had done, and his heart was full of a great joy, for Eckley had been building some additions to his house, and sent for Josh to do the plastering for him. The owner admonished his slave, took him over a few examples to freshen his memory, and sent him forth with glee. When the job was done, there was a discrepancy of two dollars in what Mr. Eckley offered for it and the price which accrued from Josh's measurements. To the employer's surprise, the black man went over the figures with him and convinced him of the incorrectness of the payment, — and the additional two dollars were turned over.

"Some o' Leckler's work," said Eckley, "teaching a nigger to cipher! Close-fisted old reprobate, — I've a mind to have the law on him." Mr. Leckler heard the story with great glee. "I laid for him that time — the old fox." But to Mrs. Leckler he said: "You see, my dear wife, my rashness in teaching Josh to figure for himself is vindicated. See what he has saved for himself."

"What did he save?" asked the little woman indiscreetly.

Her husband blushed and stammered for a moment, and then replied, "Well, of course, it was only twenty cents saved to him, but to a man buying his freedom every cent counts; and after all, it is not the amount, Mrs. Leckler, it's the principle of the thing."

"Yes," said the lady meekly.

II

Unto the body it is easy for the master to say, "Thus far shalt thou go, and no farther." Gyves, chains and fetters will enforce that command. But what master shall say unto the mind, "Here do I set the limit of your acquisition. Pass it not"? Who shall put gyves upon the intellect, or fetter the movement of thought? Joshua Leckler, as custom denominated him, had tasted of the forbidden fruit, and his appetite had grown by what it fed on. Night after night he crouched in his lonely cabin, by the blaze of a fat pine brand, poring over the few books that he had been able to secure and smuggle in. His fellow-servants alternately laughed at him and wondered why he did not take a wife. But Joshua went on his way. He had no time for marrying or for love; other thoughts had taken possession of him. He was being swayed by ambitions other than the mere fathering of slaves for his master. To him his slavery was deep night. What wonder, then, that he should dream, and that through the ivory gate should come to him the forbidden vision of freedom? To own himself, to be master of his hands, feet, of his whole body — something would clutch at his heart as he thought of it; and the breath would come hard between his lips. But he met his master with an impassive face, always silent, always docile; and Mr. Leckler congratulated himself that so valuable and intelligent a slave should be at the same time so tractable. Usually intelligence in a slave meant discontent; but not so with Josh. Who more content than he? He remarked to his wife: "You see, my dear, this is what comes of treating even a nigger right."

Meanwhile the white hills of the North were beckoning to the chattel, and the north winds were whispering to him to be a chattel no longer. Often the eyes that looked away to where freedom lay were filled with a wistful longing that was tragic in its intensity, for they saw the hardships and the difficulties between the slave and his goal and, worst of all, an iniquitous law, — liberty's compromise with bondage, that rose like a stone wall between him and hope, — a law that degraded every free-thinking man to the level of a slave-catcher. There it loomed up before him, formidable, impregnable, insurmountable. He measured it in all its terribleness, and paused. But on the other side there was liberty; and one day when he was away at work, a voice came out of the woods and whispered to him "Courage!" — and on that night the shadows beckoned him as the white hills had done, and the forest called to him, "Follow."

"It seems to me that Josh might have been able to get home tonight," said Mr. Leckler, walking up and down his veranda; "but I reckon it's just possible that he got through too late to catch a train." In the morning he said: "Well, he's not here yet; he must have had to do some extra work. If he doesn't get here by evening, I'll run up there."

In the evening, he did take the train for Joshua's place of employment, where he learned that his slave had left the night before. But where could he have gone? That no one knew, and for the first time it dawned upon his master that Josh had run away. He raged; he fumed; but nothing could be done until morning, and all the time Leckler knew that the most valuable slave on his plantation was working his way toward the North and freedom. He did not go back home, but paced the floor all night long. In the early dawn he hurried out, and the hounds were put on the fugitive's track. After some nosing around they set off toward a stretch of woods. In a few minutes they came yelping back, pawing their noses and rubbing their heads against the ground. They had found the trail, but Josh had played the old slave trick of filling his tracks with cayenne pepper. The dogs were soothed, and taken deeper into the wood to find the trail. They soon took it up again, and dashed away with low bays. The scent led them directly to a little wayside station about six miles distant. Here it stopped. Burning with the chase, Mr. Leckler hastened to the station agent. Had he seen such a negro? Yes, he had taken the northbound train two nights before.

"But why did you let him go without a pass?" almost screamed the owner.

"I didn't," replied the agent. "He had a written pass, signed James Leckler, and I let him go on it."

"Forged, forged!" yelled the master. "He wrote it himself."

"Humph!" said the agent, "how was I to know that? Our niggers round here don't know how to write."

Mr. Leckler suddenly bethought him to hold his peace. Josh was probably now in the arms of some northern abolitionist, and there was nothing to be done now but advertise; and the disgusted master spread his notices broadcast before starting for home. As soon as he arrived at his house, he sought his wife and poured out his griefs to her.

"You see, Mrs. Leckler, this is what comes of my goodness of heart. I taught that nigger to read and write, so that he could protect himself, – and look how he uses his knowledge. Oh, the ingrate, the ingrate! The very weapon which I give him to defend himself against others he turns upon me. Oh, it's awful, – awful! I've always been too confiding. Here's the most valuable nigger on my plantation gone, – gone, I tell you, – and through my own kindness. It isn't his value, though, I'm thinking so much about. I could stand his loss, if it wasn't for the principle of the thing, the base ingratitude he has shown me. Oh, if I ever lay hands on him again!" Mr. Leckler closed his lips and clenched his fist with an eloquence that laughed at words.

Just at this time, in one of the underground railway stations, six miles north of the Ohio, an old Quaker was saying to Josh: "Lie still, – thee'll be perfectly safe there. Here comes John Trader, our local slave catcher, but I will parley with him and send him away. Thee need not fear. None of thy brethren who have come to us have ever been taken back to bondage. – Good-evening, Friend Trader!" and Josh heard the old Quaker's smooth voice roll on, while he lay back half smothering in a bag, among other bags of corn and potatoes.

It was after ten o'clock that night when he was thrown carelessly into a wagon and driven away to the next station, twenty-five miles to the northward. And by such stages, hiding by day and traveling by night, helped by a few of his own people who were blessed with freedom, and always by the good Quakers wherever found, he made his way into Canada. And on one never-to-be-forgotten morning he stood up, straightened himself, breathed God's blessed air, and knew himself free!

III

To Joshua Leckler this life in Canada was all new and strange. It was a new thing for him to feel himself a man and to have his manhood recognized by the whites with whom he came into free contact. It was new, too, this receiving the full measure of his worth in work. He went to his labor with a zest that he had never known before, and he took a pleasure in the very weariness it brought him. Ever and anon there came to his ears the cries of his brethren in the South. Frequently he met fugitives who, like himself, had escaped from bondage; and the harrowing tales that they told him made him burn to do something for those whom he had left behind him. But these fugitives and the papers he read told him other things. They said that the spirit of freedom was working in the United States, and already men were speaking out boldly in behalf of the manumission of the slaves; already there was a growing army behind that noble vanguard, Sumner, Phillips, Douglass, Garrison. He heard the names of Lucretia Mott and Harriet Beecher Stowe, and his heart swelled, for on the dim horizon he saw the first faint streaks of dawn.

So the years passed. Then from the surcharged clouds a flash of lightning broke, and there was the thunder of cannon and the rain of lead over the land. From his home in the North he watched the storm as it raged and wavered, now threatening the North with its awful power, now hanging dire and dreadful over the South. Then suddenly from out the fray came a voice like the trumpet tone of God to him: "Thou and thy brothers are free!" Free, free, with the freedom not cherished by the few alone, but for all that had been bound. Free, with the freedom not torn from the secret night, but open to the light of heaven.

When the first call for colored soldiers came, Joshua Leckler hastened down to Boston, and enrolled himself among those who were willing to fight to maintain their freedom. On account of his ability to read and write and his general intelligence, he was soon made an orderly sergeant. His regiment had already taken part in an engagement before the public roster of this band of Uncle Sam's niggers, as they were called, fell into Mr. Leckler's hands. He ran his eye down the column of names. It stopped at that of Joshua Leckler, Sergeant, Company F. He handed the paper to Mrs. Leckler with his finger on the place:

"Mrs. Leckler," he said, "this is nothing less than a judgment on me for teaching a nigger to read and write. I disobeyed the law of my state and, as a result, not only lost my nigger, but furnished the Yankees with a smart officer to help them fight the South. Mrs. Leckler, I have sinned — and been punished. But I am content, Mrs. Leckler; it all came through my kindness of heart, — and your mistaken advice. But, oh, that ingrate, that ingrate!"

THE CASE OF 'CA'LINE'

A KITCHEN MONOLOGUE

The man of the house is about to go into the dining-room when he hears voices that tell him that his wife has gone down to give the "hired help" a threatened going over. He quietly withdraws, closes the door noiselessly behind him and listens from a safe point of vantage.

One voice is timid and hesitating; that is his wife. The other is fearlessly raised; that is her majesty, the queen who rules the kitchen, and from it the rest of the house.

This is what he overhears:

"Well, Mis' Ma'tin, hit do seem lak you jes' bent an' boun' to be a-fin'in' fault wid me w'en de Lawd knows I's doin' de ve'y bes' I kin. What 'bout de brekfus'? De steak too done an' de 'taters ain't done enough! Now, Miss Ma'tin, I jes' want to show you I cooked dat steak an' dem 'taters de same lengt' o' time. Seems to me dey ought to be done de same. Dat uz a thick steak, an' I jes' got hit browned thoo nice. What mo'd you want?

"You didn't want it fried at all? Now, Mis' Ma'tin, 'clah to goodness! Who evah hyeah de beat o' dat? Don't you know dat fried meat is de bes' kin' in de worl'? W'y, de las' fambly dat I lived wid — dat uz ol' Jedge Johnson — he said dat I beat anybody fryin' he evah seen; said I fried evahthing in sight, an' he said my fried food stayed by him longer than anything he evah e't. Even w'en he paid me off he said it was 'case he thought somebody else ought to have de benefit of my wunnerful powahs. Huh, ma'am, I's used to de bes'. De Jedge paid me de highes' kin' o' comperments. De las' thing he say to me was, 'Ca'line, Ca'line,' he say, 'yo' cookin' is a pa'dox. It is crim'nal, dey ain't no 'sputin' dat, but it ain't action'ble.' Co'se, I didn't unnerstan' his langidge, but I knowed hit was comperments, 'case his wife, Mis' Jedge Johnson, got right jealous an' told him to shet his mouf.

"Dah you goes. Now, who'd 'a' thought dat a lady of yo' raisin' an unnerstannin' would 'a' brung dat up. De mo'nin' you come an' ketch me settin' down an' de brekfus not ready, I was a-steadyin'. I's a mighty han' to steady, Mis' Ma'tin. 'Deed I steadies mos' all de time. But dat mo'nin' I got to steadyin' an' aftah while I sot down an' all my troubles come to my min'. I sho' has a heap o' trouble. I jes' sot thaih a-steadyin' 'bout 'em an' a-steadyin' tell bime-by, hyeah you comes.

"No, ma'am, I wasn't 'sleep. I's mighty apt to nod w'en I's a-thinkin'. It's a kin' o' keepin' time to my idees. But bless yo' soul I wasn't 'sleep. I shets my eyes so's to see to think bettah. An' aftah all, Mistah Ma'tin wasn't mo' 'n half an houah late dat mo'nin' nohow, 'case w'en I did git up I sholy flew. Ef you jes' 'membahs 'bout my steadyin' we ain't nevah gwine have no trouble long's I stays hyeah.

"You say dat one night I stayed out tell one o'clock. W'y — oh, yes. Dat uz Thu'sday night. W'y la! Mis' Ma'tin, dat's de night my s'ciety meets, de Af'Ame'ican Sons an' Daughtahs of Judah. We had to 'nitianate a new can'date dat night, an' la! I wish you'd 'a' been thaih, you'd 'a' killed yo'self a-laffin'.

"You nevah did see sich ca'in's on in all yo' bo'n days. It was pow'ful funny. Broth' Eph'am Davis, he's ouah Mos' Wusshipful Rabbi, he says hit uz de mos' s'cessful 'nitination we evah had. Dat can'date pawed de groun' lak a hoss an' tried to git outen de winder. But I got to be mighty keerful how I talk: I do' know whethah you 'long to any secut s'cieties er not. I wouldn't been so late even fu' dat, but Mistah Hi'am Smif, he gallanted me home an' you know a lady boun' to stan' at de gate an' talk to huh comp'ny a little while. You know how it is, Mis' Ma'tin.

"I been en'tainin' my comp'ny in de pa'lor? Co'se I has; you wasn't usin' it. What you s'pose my frien's 'u'd think ef I'd ax 'em in de kitchen w'en dey wasn't no one in de front room? Co'se I ax 'em in de pa'lor. I do' want my frien's to think I's wo'kin' fu' no low-down people. W'y, Miss 'Liza Harris set down an' played mos' splendid on yo' pianna, an' she compermented you mos' high. S'pose I'd a tuck huh in de kitchen, whaih de comperments come in?

"Yass'm, yass'm, I does tek home little things now an' den, dat I does, an' I ain't gwine to 'ny it. I jes' says to myse'f, I ain't wo'kin' fu' no strainers lak de people nex' do', what goes into tantrums ef de lady what cooks fu' 'em teks home a bit o' sugar. I 'lows to myse'f I ain't wo'kin' fu' no sich folks; so sometimes I teks home jes' a weenchy bit o' somep'n' dat nobody couldn't want nohow, an' I knows you ain't gwine 'ject to dat. You do 'ject, you do 'ject! Huh!

"I's got to come an' ax you, has I? Look a-hyeah, Mis' Ma'tin, I know I has to wo'k in yo' kitchen. I know I has to cook fu' you, but I want you to know dat even ef I does I's a lady. I's a lady, but I see you do' know how to 'preciate a lady w'en you meets one. You kin jes' light in an' git yo' own dinner. I wouldn't wo'k fu' you ef you uz made o' gol'. I nevah did lak to wo'k fu' strainers, nohow.

"No, ma'am, I cain't even stay an' git de dinner. I know w'en I been insulted. Seems lak ef I stay in hyeah another minute I'll bile all over dis kitchen.

"Who excited? Me excited? No, I ain't excited. I's mad. I do' lak nobody pesterin' 'roun' my kitchen, nohow, huh, uh, honey. Too many places in dis town waitin' fu' Ca'line Mason.

"No, indeed, you needn't 'pologize to me! needn't 'pologize to me. I b'lieve in people sayin' jes' what dey mean, I does.

"Would I stay, ef you 'crease my wages? Well — I reckon I could, but I — but I do' want no foolishness."

(Sola.) "Huh! Did she think she was gwine to come down hyeah an' skeer me, huh, uh? Whaih's dat fryin' pan?"

The man of the house hears the rustle of his wife's skirts as she beats a retreat and he goes upstairs and into the library whistling, "See, the Conquering Hero Comes."

THE FINISH OF PATSY BARNES

His name was Patsy Barnes, and he was a denizen of Little Africa. In fact, he lived on Douglass Street. By all the laws governing the relations between people and their names, he should have been Irish — but he was not. He was colored, and very much so. That was the reason he lived on Douglass Street. The negro has very strong within him the instinct of colonization and it was in accordance with this that Patsy's mother had found her way to Little Africa when she had come North from Kentucky.

Patsy was incorrigible. Even into the confines of Little Africa had penetrated the truant officer and the terrible penalty of the compulsory education law. Time and time again had poor Eliza Barnes been brought up on account of the shortcomings of that son of hers. She was a hard-working, honest woman, and day by day bent over her tub, scrubbing away to keep Patsy in shoes and jackets, that would wear out so much faster than they could be bought. But she never murmured, for she loved the boy with a deep affection, though his misdeeds were a sore thorn in her side.

She wanted him to go to school. She wanted him to learn. She had the notion that he might become something better, something higher than she had been. But for him school had no charms; his school was the cool stalls in the big livery stable near at hand; the arena of his pursuits its sawdust floor; the height of his ambition, to be a horseman. Either here or in the racing stables at the Fair-grounds he spent his truant hours. It was a school that taught much, and Patsy was as apt a pupil as he was a constant attendant. He learned strange things about horses, and fine, sonorous oaths that sounded eerie on his young lips, for he had only turned into his fourteenth year.

A man goes where he is appreciated; then could this slim black boy be blamed for doing the same thing? He was a great favorite with the horsemen, and picked up many a dime or nickel for dancing or singing, or even a quarter for warming up a horse for its owner. He was not to be blamed for this, for, first of all, he was born in Kentucky, and had spent the very days of his infancy about the paddocks near Lexington, where his father had sacrificed his life on account of his love for horses. The little fellow had shed no tears when he looked at his father's bleeding body, bruised and broken by the fiery young two-year-old he was trying to subdue. Patsy did not sob or whimper, though his heart ached, for over all the feeling of his grief was a mad, burning desire to ride that horse.

His tears were shed, however, when, actuated by the idea that times would be easier up North, they moved to Dalesford. Then, when he learned that he must leave his old friends, the horses and their masters, whom he had known, he wept. The comparatively meagre appointments of the Fairgrounds at Dalesford proved a poor compensation for all these. For the first few weeks Patsy had dreams of running away — back to Kentucky and the horses and stables. Then after a while he settled himself with heroic resolution to make the best of what he had, and with a mighty effort took up the burden of life away from his beloved home.

Eliza Barnes, older and more experienced though she was, took up her burden with a less cheerful philosophy than her son. She worked hard, and made a scanty livelihood, it is true, but she did not make the best of what she had. Her complainings were loud in the land, and her wailings for her old home smote the ears of any who would listen to her.

They had been living in Dalesford for a year nearly, when hard work and exposure brought the woman down to bed with pneumonia. They were very poor — too poor even to call in a doctor, so there was nothing to do but to call in the city physician. Now this medical man had too frequent calls into Little Africa, and he did not like to go there. So he was very gruff when any of its denizens called him, and it was even said that he was careless of his patients.

Patsy's heart bled as he heard the doctor talking to his mother:

"Now, there can't be any foolishness about this," he said. "You've got to stay in bed and not get yourself damp."

"How long you think I got to lay hyeah, doctah?" she asked.

"I'm a doctor, not a fortune-teller," was the reply. "You'll lie there as long as the disease holds you."

"But I can't lay hyeah long, doctah, case I ain't got nuffin' to go on."

"Well, take your choice: the bed or the boneyard."

Eliza began to cry.

"You needn't sniffle," said the doctor; "I don't see what you people want to come up here for anyhow. Why don't you stay down South where you belong? You come up here and you're just a burden and a trouble to the city. The South deals with all of you better, both in poverty and crime." He knew that these people did not understand him, but he wanted an outlet for the heat within him.

There was another angry being in the room, and that was Patsy. His eyes were full of tears that scorched him and would not fall. The memory of many beautiful and appropriate oaths came to him; but he dared not let his mother hear him swear. Oh! to have a stone — to be across the street from that man!

When the physician walked out, Patsy went to the bed, took his mother's hand, and bent over shamefacedly to kiss her. He did not know that with that act the Recording Angel blotted out many a curious damn of his.

The little mark of affection comforted Eliza unspeakably. The mother-feeling overwhelmed her in one burst of tears. Then she dried her eyes and smiled at him.

"Honey," she said; "mammy ain' gwine lay hyeah long. She be all right putty soon."

"Nevah you min'," said Patsy with a choke in his voice. "I can do somep'n', an' we'll have anothah doctah."

"La, listen at de chile; what kin you do?"

"I'm goin' down to McCarthy's stable and see if I kin git some horses to exercise."

A sad look came into Eliza's eyes as she said: "You'd bettah not go, Patsy; dem hosses'll kill you yit, des lak dey did yo' pappy."

But the boy, used to doing pretty much as he pleased, was obdurate, and even while she was talking, put on his ragged jacket and left the room.

Patsy was not wise enough to be diplomatic. He went right to the point with McCarthy, the liveryman.

The big red-faced fellow slapped him until he spun round and round. Then he said, "Ye little devil, ye, I've a mind to knock the whole head off o' ye. Ye want harses to exercise, do ye? Well git on that 'un, an' see what ye kin do with him."

The boy's honest desire to be helpful had tickled the big, generous Irishman's peculiar sense of humor, and from now on, instead of giving Patsy a horse to ride now and then as he had formerly done, he put into his charge all the animals that needed exercise.

It was with a king's pride that Patsy marched home with his first considerable earnings.

They were small yet, and would go for food rather than a doctor, but Eliza was inordinately proud, and it was this pride that gave her strength and the desire of life to carry her through the days approaching the crisis of her disease.

As Patsy saw his mother growing worse, saw her gasping for breath, heard the rattling as she drew in the little air that kept going her clogged lungs, felt the heat of her burning hands, and saw the pitiful appeal in her poor eyes, he became convinced that the city doctor was not helping her. She must have another. But the money?

That afternoon, after his work with McCarthy, found him at the Fair-grounds. The spring races were on, and he thought he might get a job warming up the horse of some independent jockey. He hung around the stables, listening to the talk of men he knew and some he had never seen before. Among the latter was a tall, lanky man, holding forth to a group of men.

"No, suh," he was saying to them generally, "I'm goin' to withdraw my hoss, because thaih ain't nobody to ride him as he ought to be rode. I haven't brought a jockey along with me, so I've got to depend on pick-ups. Now, the talent's set agin my hoss, Black Boy, because he's been losin' regular, but that hoss has lost for the want of ridin', that's all."

The crowd looked in at the slim-legged, raw-boned horse, and walked away laughing.

"The fools!" muttered the stranger. "If I could ride myself I'd show 'em!"

Patsy was gazing into the stall at the horse.

"What are you doing thaih," called the owner to him.

"Look hyeah, mistah," said Patsy, "ain't that a bluegrass hoss?"

"Of co'se it is, an' one o' the fastest that evah grazed."

"I'll ride that hoss, mistah."

"What do you know 'bout ridin'?"

"I used to gin'ally be' roun' Mistah Boone's paddock in Lexington, an' —"

"Aroun' Boone's paddock — what! Look here, little nigger, if you can ride that hoss to a winnin' I'll give you more money than you ever seen before."

"I'll ride him."

Patsy's heart was beating very wildly beneath his jacket. That horse. He knew that glossy coat. He knew that raw-boned frame and those flashing nostrils. That black horse there owed something to the orphan he had made.

The horse was to ride in the race before the last. Somehow out of odds and ends, his owner scraped together a suit and colors for Patsy. The colors were maroon and green, a curious combination. But then it was a curious horse, a curious rider, and a more curious combination that brought the two together.

Long before the time for the race Patsy went into the stall to become better acquainted with his horse. The animal turned its wild eyes upon him and neighed. He patted the long, slender head, and grinned as the horse stepped aside as gently as a lady.

"He sholy is full o' ginger," he said to the owner, whose name he had found to be Brackett.

"He'll show 'em a thing or two," laughed Brackett.

"His dam was a fast one," said Patsy, unconsciously.

Brackett whirled on him in a flash. "What do you know about his dam?"

he asked.

The boy would have retracted, but it was too late. Stammeringly he told the story of his father's death and the horse's connection therewith.

"Well," said Brackett, "if you don't turn out a hoodoo, you're a winner, sure. But I'll be blessed if this don't sound like a story! But I've heard that story before. The man I got Black Boy from, no matter how I got him, you're too young to understand the ins and outs of poker, told it to me."

When the bell sounded and Patsy went out to warm up, he felt as if he were riding on air. Some of the jockeys laughed at his get-up, but there was something in him — or under him, maybe — that made him scorn their derision. He saw a sea of faces about him, then saw no more. Only a shining white track loomed ahead of him, and a restless steed was cantering with him around the curve. Then the bell called him back to the stand.

They did not get away at first, and back they trooped. A second trial was a failure. But at the third they were off in a line as straight as a chalk-mark. There were Essex and Firefly, Queen Bess and Mosquito, galloping away side by side, and Black Boy a neck ahead. Patsy knew the family reputation of his horse for endurance as well as fire, and began riding the race from the first. Black Boy came of blood that would not be passed, and to this his rider trusted. At the eighth the line was hardly broken, but as the quarter was reached Black Boy had forged a length ahead, and Mosquito was at his flank. Then, like a flash, Essex shot out ahead under whip and spur, his jockey standing straight in the stirrups.

The crowd in the stand screamed; but Patsy smiled as he lay low over his horse's neck. He saw that Essex had made her best spurt. His only fear was for Mosquito, who hugged and hugged his flank. They were nearing the three-quarter post, and he was tightening his grip on the black. Essex fell back; his spurt was over. The whip fell unheeded on his sides. The spurs dug him in vain.

Black Boy's breath touches the leader's ear. They are neck and neck — nose to nose. The black stallion passes him.

Another cheer from the stand, and again Patsy smiles as they turn into the stretch. Mosquito has gained a head. The colored boy flashes one glance at the horse and rider who are so surely gaining upon him, and his lips close in a grim line. They are halfway down the stretch, and Mosquito's head is at the stallion's neck.

For a single moment Patsy thinks of the sick woman at home and what that race will mean to her, and then his knees close against the horse's sides with a firmer dig. The spurs shoot deeper into the steaming flanks. Black Boy shall win; he must win. The horse that has taken away his father shall give him back his mother. The stallion leaps away like a flash, and goes under the wire — a length ahead.

Then the band thundered, and Patsy was off his horse, very warm and very happy, following his mount to the stable. There, a little later, Brackett found him. He rushed to him, and flung his arms around him.

"You little devil," he cried, "you rode like you were kin to that hoss! We've won! We've won!" And he began sticking banknotes at the boy. At first Patsy's eyes bulged, and then he seized the money and got into his clothes.

"Goin' out to spend it?" asked Brackett.

"I'm goin' for a doctah fu' my mother," said Patsy, "she's sick."

"Don't let me lose sight of you."

"Oh, I'll see you again. So long," said the boy.

An hour later he walked into his mother's room with a very big doctor, the greatest the druggist could direct him to. The doctor left his medicines and his orders, but, when Patsy told his story, it was Eliza's pride that started her on the road to recovery. Patsy did not tell his horse's name.

ONE MAN'S FORTUNES

PART I

When Bertram Halliday left the institution which, in the particular part of the middle west where he was born, was called the state university, he did not believe, as young graduates are reputed to, that he had conquered the world and had only to come into his kingdom. He knew that the battle of life was, in reality, just beginning and, with a common sense unusual to his twenty-three years but born out of the exigencies of a none-too-easy life, he recognized that for him the battle would be harder than for his white comrades.

Looking at his own position, he saw himself the member of a race dragged from complacent savagery into the very heat and turmoil of a civilization for which it was in nowise prepared; bowed beneath a yoke to which its shoulders were not fitted, and then, without warning, thrust forth into a freedom as absurd as it was startling and overwhelming. And yet, he felt, as most young men must feel, an individual strength that would exempt him from the workings of the general law. His outlook on life was calm and unfrightened. Because he knew the dangers that beset his way, he feared them less. He felt assured because with so clear an eye he saw the weak places in his armor which the world he was going to meet would attack, and these he was prepared to strengthen. Was it not the fault of youth and self-confessed weakness, he thought, to go into the world always thinking of it as a foe? Was not this great Cosmopolis, this dragon of a thousand talons kind as well as cruel? Had it not friends as well as enemies? Yes. That was it: the outlook of young men, of colored young men in particular, was all wrong, — they had gone at the world in the wrong spirit. They had looked upon it as a terrible foeman and forced it to be one. He would do it, oh, so differently. He would take the world as a friend. He would even take the old, old world under his wing.

They sat in the room talking that night, he and Webb Davis and Charlie McLean. It was the last night they were to be together in so close a relation. The commencement was over. They had their sheepskins. They were pitched there on the bed very carelessly to be the important things they were, — the reward of four years digging in Greek and Mathematics.

They had stayed after the exercises of the day just where they had first stopped. This was at McLean's rooms, dismantled and topsy-turvy with the business of packing. The pipes were going and the talk kept pace. Old men smoke slowly and in great whiffs with long intervals of silence between their observations. Young men draw fast and say many and bright things, for young men are wise, — while they are young.

"Now, it's just like this," Davis was saying to McLean, "Here we are, all three of us turned out into the world like a lot of little sparrows pitched out of the nest, and what are we going to do? Of course it's easy enough for you, McLean, but what are my grave friend with the nasty black briar, and I, your humble servant, to do? In what wilderness are we to pitch our tents and where is our manna coming from?"

"Oh, well, the world owes us all a living," said McLean.

"Hackneyed, but true. Of course it does; but every time a colored man goes around to collect, the world throws up its hands and yells 'insolvent' — eh, Halliday?"

Halliday took his pipe from his mouth as if he were going to say something. Then he put it back without speaking and looked meditatively through the blue smoke.

"I'm right," Davis went on, "to begin with, we colored people haven't any show here. Now, if we could go to Central or South America, or some place like that, — but hang it all, who wants to go thousands of miles away from home to earn a little bread and butter?"

"There's India and the young Englishmen, if I remember rightly," said McLean.

"Oh, yes, that's all right, with the Cabots and Drake and Sir John Franklin behind them. Their traditions, their blood, all that they know makes them willing to go 'where there ain't no ten commandments and a man can raise a thirst,' but for me, home, if I can call it home."

"Well, then, stick it out."

"That's easy enough to say, McLean; but ten to one you've got some snap picked out for you already, now 'fess up, ain't you?"

"Well, of course I'm going in with my father, I can't help that, but I've got —"

"To be sure," broke in Davis, "you go in with your father. Well, if all I had to do was to step right out of college into my father's business with an assured salary, however small, I shouldn't be falling on my own neck and weeping tonight. But that's just the trouble with us; we haven't got fathers before us or behind us, if you'd rather."

"More luck to you, you'll be a father before or behind some one else; you'll be an ancestor."

"It's more profitable being a descendant, I find."

A glow came into McLean's face and his eyes sparkled as he replied: "Why, man, if I could, I'd change places with you. You don't deserve your fate. What is before you? Hardships, perhaps, and long waiting. But then, you have the zest of the fight, the joy of the action and the chance of conquering. Now what is before me, — me, whom you are envying? I go out of here into a dull counting-room. The way is prepared for me. Perhaps I shall have no hardships, but neither have I the joy that comes from pains endured. Perhaps I shall have no battle, but even so, I lose the pleasure of the fight and the glory of winning. Your fate is infinitely to be preferred to mine."

"Ah, now you talk with the voluminous voice of the centuries," bantered Davis. "You are but echoing the breath of your Nelsons, your Cabots, your Drakes and your Franklins. Why, can't you see, you sentimental idiot, that it's all different and has to be different with us? The Anglo-Saxon race has been producing that fine frenzy in you for seven centuries and more. You come, with the blood of merchants, pioneers and heroes in your veins, to a normal battle. But for me, my forebears were savages two hundred years ago. My people learn to know civilization by the lowest and most degrading contact with it, and thus equipped or unequipped I tempt, an abnormal contest. Can't you see the disproportion?"

"If I do, I can also see the advantage of it."

"For the sake of common sense, Halliday," said Davis, turning to his companion, "don't sit there like a clam; open up and say something to convince this Don Quixote who, because he himself, sees only windmills, cannot be persuaded that we have real dragons to fight."

"Do you fellows know Henley?" asked Halliday, with apparent irrelevance.

"I know him as a critic," said McLean.

"I know him as a name," echoed the worldly Davis, "but —"

"I mean his poems," resumed Halliday, "he is the most virile of the present-day poets. Kipling is virile, but he gives you the man in hot blood with the brute in him to the fore; but the strong masculinity of Henley is essentially intellectual. It is the mind that is conquering always."

"Well, now that you have settled the relative place in English letters of Kipling and Henley, might I be allowed humbly to ask what in the name of all that is good has that to do with the question before the house?"

"I don't know your man's poetry," said McLean, "but I do believe that I can see what you are driving at."

"Wonderful perspicacity, oh, youth!"

"If Webb will agree not to run, I'll spring on you the poem that seems to me to strike the keynote of the matter in hand."

"Oh, well, curiosity will keep me. I want to get your position, and I want to see McLean annihilated."

In a low, even tone, but without attempt at dramatic effect, Halliday began to recite:

"Out of the night that covers me,
Black as the pit from pole to pole,
I thank whatever gods there be
For my unconquerable soul!

"In the fell clutch of circumstance,
I have not winced nor cried aloud.
Under the bludgeonings of chance,
My head is bloody, but unbowed.

"Beyond this place of wrath and tears
Looms but the horror of the shade,
And yet the menace of the years
Finds, and shall find me unafraid.

"It matters not how strait the gate,
How charged with punishments the scroll,
I am the master of my fate,
I am the captain of my soul."

"That's it," exclaimed McLean, leaping to his feet, "that's what I mean. That's the sort of a stand for a man to take."

Davis rose and knocked the ashes from his pipe against the window-sill. "Well, for two poetry-spouting, poetry-consuming, sentimental idiots, commend me to you fellows. Master of my fate, captain of my soul, be dashed! Old Jujube, with his bone-pointed hunting spear, began determining a couple of hundred years ago what I should be in this year of our Lord one thousand eight hundred and ninety-four. J. Webb Davis, senior, added another brick to this structure, when he was picking cotton on his master's plantation forty years ago."

"And now," said Halliday, also rising, "don't you think it fair that you should start out with the idea of adding a few bricks of your own, and all of a better make than those of your remote ancestor, Jujube, or that nearer one, your father?"

"Spoken like a man," said McLean.

"Oh, you two are so hopelessly young," laughed Davis.

PART II

After the two weeks' rest which he thought he needed, and consequently promised himself, Halliday began to look about him for some means of making a start for that success in life which he felt so sure of winning.

With this end in view he returned to the town where he was born. He had settled upon the law as a profession, and had studied it for a year or two while at college. He would go back to Broughton now to pursue his studies, but of course, he needed money. No difficulty, however, presented itself in the getting of this for he knew several fellows who had been able to go into offices, and by collecting and similar duties make something while they studied. Webb Davis would have said, "but they were white," but Halliday knew what his own reply would have been: "What a white man can do, I can do."

Even if he could not go to studying at once, he could go to work and save enough money to go on with his course in a year or two. He had lots of time before him, and he only needed a little start. What better place then, to go to than Broughton, where he had first seen the light? Broughton, that had known him, boy and man. Broughton that had watched him through the common school and the high school, and had seen him go off to college with some pride and a good deal of curiosity. For even in middle west towns of such a size, that is, between seventy and eighty thousand souls, a "smart negro" was still a freak.

So Halliday went back home because the people knew him there and would respect his struggles and encourage his ambitions.

He had been home two days, and the old town had begun to take on its remembered aspect as he wandered through the streets and along the river banks. On this second day he was going up Main street deep in a brown study when he heard his name called by a young man who was approaching him, and saw an outstretched hand.

"Why, how de do, Bert, how are you? Glad to see you back. I hear you have been astonishing them up at college."

Halliday's reverie had been so suddenly broken into that for a moment, the young fellow's identity wavered elusively before his mind and then it materialized, and his consciousness took hold of it. He remembered him, not as an intimate, but as an acquaintance whom he had often met upon the football and baseball fields.

"How do you do? It's Bob Dickson," he said, shaking the proffered hand, which at the mention of the name, had grown unaccountably cold in his grasp.

"Yes, I'm Mr. Dickson," said the young man, patronizingly. "You seem to have developed wonderfully, you hardly seem like the same Bert Halliday I used to know."

"Yes, but I'm the same Mr. Halliday."

"Oh — ah — yes," said the young man, "well, I'm glad to have seen you. Ah — good-bye, Bert."

"Good-bye, Bob."

"Presumptuous darky!" murmured Mr. Dickson.

"Insolent puppy!" said Mr. Halliday to himself.

But the incident made no impression on his mind as bearing upon his status in the public eye. He only thought the fellow a cad, and went hopefully on. He was rather amused than otherwise. In this frame of mind, he turned into one of the large office-buildings that lined the street and made his way to a business suite over whose door was the inscription, "H.G. Featherton, Counsellor and Attorney-at-Law." Mr. Featherton had shown considerable interest in Bert in his school days, and he hoped much from him.

As he entered the public office, a man sitting at the large desk in the centre of the room turned and faced him. He was a fair man of an indeterminate age, for you could not tell whether those were streaks of grey shining in his light hair, or only the glint which it took on in the sun. His face was dry, lean and intellectual. He smiled now and then, and his smile was like a flash of winter lightning, so cold and quick it was. It went as suddenly as it came, leaving the face as marbly cold and impassive as ever. He rose and extended his hand, "Why — why — ah — Bert, how de do, how are you?"

"Very well, I thank you, Mr. Featherton."

"Hum, I'm glad to see you back, sit down. Going to stay with us, you think?"

"I'm not sure, Mr. Featherton; it all depends upon my getting something to do."

"You want to go to work, do you? Hum, well, that's right. It's work makes the man. What do you propose to do, now since you've graduated?"

Bert warmed at the evident interest of his old friend. "Well, in the first place, Mr. Featherton," he replied, "I must get to work and make some money. I have heard of fellows studying and supporting themselves at the same time, but I musn't expect too much. I'm going to study law."

The attorney had schooled his face into hiding any emotion he might feel, and it did not betray him now. He only flashed one of his quick cold smiles and asked,

"Don't you think you've taken rather a hard profession to get on in?"

"No doubt. But anything I should take would be hard. It's just like this, Mr. Featherton," he went on, "I am willing to work and to work hard, and I am not looking for any snap."

Mr. Featherton was so unresponsive to this outburst that Bert was ashamed of it the minute it left his lips. He wished this man would not be so cold and polite and he wished he would stop putting the ends of his white fingers together as carefully as if something depended upon it.

"I say the law is a hard profession to get on in, and as a friend I say that it will be harder for you. Your people have not the money to spend in litigation of any kind."

"I should not cater for the patronage of my own people alone."

"Yes, but the time has not come when a white person will employ a colored attorney."

"Do you mean to say that the prejudice here at home is such that if I were as competent as a white lawyer a white person would not employ me?"

"I say nothing about prejudice at all. It's nature. They have their own lawyers; why should they go outside of their own to employ a colored man?"

"But I am of their own. I am an American citizen, there should be no thought of color about it."

"Oh, my boy, that theory is very nice, but State University democracy doesn't obtain in real life."

"More's the pity, then, for real life."

"Perhaps, but we must take things as we find them, not as we think they ought to be. You people are having and will have for the next ten or a dozen years the hardest fight of your lives. The sentiment of remorse and the desire for atoning which actuated so many white men to help negroes right after the war has passed off without being replaced by that sense of plain justice which gives a black man his due, not because of, nor in spite of, but without consideration of his color."

"I wonder if it can be true, as my friend Davis says, that a colored man must do twice as much and twice as well as a white man before he can hope for even equal chances with him? That white mediocrity demands black genius to cope with it?"

"I am afraid your friend has philosophized the situation about right."

"Well, we have dealt in generalities," said Bert, smiling, "let us take up the particular and personal part of this matter. Is there any way you could help me to a situation?"

"Well, — I should be glad to see you get on, Bert, but as you see, I have nothing in my office that you could do. Now, if you don't mind beginning at the bottom —"

"That's just what I expected to do."

" — Why I could speak to the head-waiter of the hotel where I stay. He's a very nice colored man and I have some influence with him. No doubt Charlie could give you a place."

"But that's a work I abhor."

"Yes, but you must begin at the bottom, you know. All young men must."

"To be sure, but would you have recommended the same thing to your nephew on his leaving college?"

"Ah — ah — that's different."

"Yes," said Halliday, rising, "it is different. There's a different bottom at which black and white young men should begin, and by a logical sequence, a different top to which they should aspire. However, Mr. Featherton, I'll ask you to hold your offer in abeyance. If I can find nothing else, I'll ask you to speak to the head-waiter. Good-morning."

"I'll do so with pleasure," said Mr. Featherton, "and good-morning."

As the young man went up the street, an announcement card in the window of a publishing house caught his eye. It was the announcement of the next Sunday's number in a series of addresses which the local business men were giving before the Y.M.C.A. It read, "'How a Christian young man can get on in the law' — an address by a Christian lawyer — H.G. Featherton."

Bert laughed. "I should like to hear that address," he said. "I wonder if he'll recommend them to his head-waiter. No, 'that's different.' All the addresses and all the books written on how to get on, are written for white men. We blacks must solve the question for ourselves."

He had lost some of the ardor with which he had started out but he was still full of hope. He refused to accept Mr. Featherton's point of view as general or final. So he hailed a passing car that in the course of a half hour set him down at the door of the great factory which, with its improvements, its army of clerks and employees, had built up one whole section of the town. He felt especially hopeful in attacking this citadel, because they were constantly advertising for clerks and their placards plainly stated that preference would be given to graduates of the local high school. The owners were philanthropists in their way. Well, what better chance could there be before him? He had graduated there and stood well in his classes, and besides, he knew that a number of his classmates were holding good positions in the factory. So his voice was cheerful as he asked to see Mr. Stockard, who had charge of the clerical department.

Mr. Stockard was a fat, wheezy young man, with a reputation for humor based entirely upon his size and his rubicund face, for he had really never said anything humorous in his life. He came panting into the room now with a "Well, what can I do for you?"

"I wanted to see you about a situation" — began Halliday.

"Oh, no, no, you don't want to see me," broke in Stockard, "you want to see the head janitor."

"But I don't want to see the head janitor. I want to see the head of the clerical department."

"You want to see the head of the clerical department!"

"Yes, sir, I see you are advertising for clerks with preference given to the high school boys. Well, I am an old high school boy, but have been away for a few years at college."

Mr. Stockard opened his eyes to their widest extent, and his jaw dropped. Evidently he had never come across such presumption before.

"We have nothing for you," he wheezed after awhile.

"Very well, I should be glad to drop in again and see you," said Halliday, moving to the door. "I hope you will remember me if anything opens."

Mr. Stockard did not reply to this or to Bert's good-bye. He stood in the middle of the floor and stared at the door through which the colored man had gone, then he dropped into a chair with a gasp.

"Well, I'm dumbed!" he said.

A doubt had begun to arise in Bertram Halliday's mind that turned him cold and then hot with a burning indignation. He could try nothing more that morning. It had brought him nothing but rebuffs. He hastened home and threw himself down on the sofa to try and think out his situation.

"Do they still require of us bricks without straw? I thought all that was over. Well, I suspect that I will have to ask Mr. Featherton to speak to his head-waiter in my behalf. I wonder if the head-waiter will demand my diploma. Webb Davis, you were nearer right than I thought."

He spent the day in the house thinking and planning.

PART III

Halliday was not a man to be discouraged easily, and for the next few weeks he kept up an unflagging search for work. He found that there were more Feathertons and Stockards than he had ever looked to find. Everywhere that he turned his face, anything but the most menial work was denied him. He thought once of going away from Broughton, but would he find it any better anywhere else, he asked himself? He determined to stay and fight it out there for two reasons. First, because he held that it would be cowardice to run away, and secondly, because he felt that he was not fighting a local disease, but was bringing the force of his life to bear upon a national evil. Broughton was as good a place to begin curative measures as elsewhere.

There was one refuge which was open to him, and which he fought against with all his might. For years now, from as far back as he could remember, the colored graduates had "gone South to teach." This course was now recommended to him. Indeed, his own family quite approved of it, and when he still stood out against the scheme, people began to say that Bertram Halliday did not want work; he wanted to be a gentleman.

But Halliday knew that the South had plenty of material, and year by year was raising and training her own teachers. He knew that the time would come, if it were not present when it would be impossible to go South to teach, and he felt it to be essential that the North should be trained in a manner looking to the employment of her own negroes. So he stayed. But he was only human, and when the tide of talk anent his indolence began to ebb and flow about him, he availed himself of the only expedient that could arrest it.

When he went back to the great factory where he had seen and talked with Mr. Stockard, he went around to another door and this time asked for the head janitor. This individual, a genial Irishman, took stock of Halliday at a glance.

"But what do ye want to be doin' sich wurruk for, whin ye've been through school?" he asked.

"I am doing the only thing I can get to do," was the answer.

"Well," said the Irishman, "ye've got sinse, anyhow."

Bert found himself employed as an under janitor at the factory at a wage of nine dollars a week. At this, he could pay his share to keep the house going, and save a little for the period of study he still looked forward to. The people who had accused him of laziness now made a martyr of him, and said what a pity it was for a man with such an education and with so much talent to be so employed menially.

He did not neglect his studies, but read at night, whenever the day's work had not made both brain and body too weary for the task.

In this way his life went along for over a year when one morning a note from Mr. Featherton summoned him to that gentleman's office. It is true that Halliday read the note with some trepidation. His bitter experience had not yet taught him how not to dream. He was not yet old enough for that. "Maybe," he thought, "Mr. Featherton has relented, and is going to give me a chance anyway. Or perhaps he wanted me to prove my metal before he consented to take me up. Well, I've tried to do it, and if that's what he wanted, I hope he's satisfied." The note which seemed written all over with joyful tidings shook in his hand.

The genial manner with which Mr. Featherton met him reaffirmed in his mind the belief that at last the lawyer had determined to give him a chance. He was almost deferential as he asked Bert into his private office, and shoved a chair forward for him.

"Well, you've been getting on, I see," he began.

"Oh, yes," replied Bert, "I have been getting on by hook and crook."

"Hum, done any studying lately?"

"Yes, but not as much as I wish to. Coke and Wharton aren't any clearer to a head grown dizzy with bending over mops, brooms and heavy trucks all day."

"No, I should think not. Ah — oh — well, Bert, how should you like to come into my office and help around, do such errands as I need and help copy my papers?"

"I should be delighted."

"It would only pay you five dollars a week, less than what you are getting now, I suppose, but it will be more genteel."

"Oh, now, that I have had to do it, I don't care so much about the lack of gentility of my present work, but I prefer what you offer because I shall have a greater chance to study."

"Well, then, you may as well come in on Monday. The office will be often in your charge, as I am going to be away a great deal in the next few months. You know I am going to make the fight for nomination to the seat on the bench which is vacant this fall."

"Indeed. I have not so far taken much interest in politics, but I will do all in my power to help you with both nomination and election."

"Thank you," said Mr. Featherton, "I am sure you can be of great service to me as the vote of your people is pretty heavy in Broughton. I have always been a friend to them, and I believe I can depend upon their support. I shall be glad of any good you can do me with them."

Bert laughed when he was out on the street again. "For value received," he said. He thought less of Mr. Featherton's generosity since he saw it was actuated by self-interest alone, but that in no wise destroyed the real worth of the opportunity that was now given into his hands. Featherton, he believed, would make an excellent judge, and he was glad that in working for his nomination his convictions so aptly fell in with his inclinations.

His work at the factory had put him in touch with a larger number of his people than he could have possibly met had he gone into the office at once. Over them, his naturally bright mind exerted some influence. As a simple laborer he had fellowshipped with them but they acknowledged and availed themselves of his leadership, because they felt instinctively in him a power which they did not have. Among them now he worked sedulously. He held that the greater part of the battle would be in the primaries, and on the night when they convened, he had his friends out in force in every ward which went to make up the third judicial district. Men who had never seen the inside of a primary meeting before were there actively engaged in this.

The *Diurnal* said next morning that the active interest of the hard-working, church-going colored voters, who wanted to see a Christian judge on the bench had had much to do with the nomination of Mr. Featherton.

The success at the primaries did not tempt Halliday to relinquish his efforts on his employer's behalf. He was indefatigable in his cause. On the west side where the colored population had largely colonized, he made speeches and held meetings clear up to election day. The fight had been between two factions of the party and after the nomination it was feared that the defection of the part defeated in the primaries might prevent the ratification of the nominee at the polls. But before the contest was half over all fears for him were laid. What he had lost in the districts where the skulking faction was strong, he made up in the wards where the colored vote was large. He was overwhelmingly elected.

Halliday smiled as he sat in the office and heard the congratulations poured in upon Judge Featherton.

"Well, it's wonderful," said one of his visitors, "how the colored boys stood by you."

"Yes, I have been a friend to the colored people, and they know it," said Featherton.

It would be some months before His Honor would take his seat on the bench, and during that time, Halliday hoped to finish his office course.

He was surprised when Featherton came to him a couple of weeks after the election and said, "Well, Bert, I guess I can get along now. I'll be shutting up this office pretty soon. Here are your wages and here is a little gift I wish to add out of respect to you for your kindness during my run for office."

Bert took the wages, but the added ten dollar note he waved aside. "No, I thank you, Mr. Featherton," he said, "what I did, I did from a belief in your fitness for the place, and out of loyalty to my employer. I don't want any money for it."

"Then let us say that I have raised your wages to this amount."

"No, that would only be evasion. I want no more than you promised to give me."

"Very well, then accept my thanks, anyway."

What things he had at the office Halliday took away that night. A couple of days later he remembered a book which he had failed to get and returned for it. The office was as usual. Mr. Featherton was a little embarrassed and nervous. At Halliday's desk sat a young white man about his own age. He was copying a deed for Mr. Featherton.

PART IV

Bertram Halliday went home, burning with indignation at the treatment he had received at the hands of the Christian judge.

"He has used me as a housemaid would use a lemon," he said, "squeezed all out of me he could get, and then flung me into the street. Well, Webb was nearer right than I thought."

He was now out of everything. His place at the factory had been filled, and no new door opened to him. He knew what reward a search for work brought a man of his color in Broughton so he did not bestir himself to go over the old track again. He thanked his stars that he, at least, had money enough to carry him away from the place and he determined to go. His spirit was quelled, but not broken.

Just before leaving, he wrote to Davis.

"My dear Webb!" the letter ran, "you, after all, were right. We have little or no show in the fight for life among these people. I have struggled for two years here at Broughton, and now find myself back where I was when I first stepped out of school with a foolish faith in being equipped for something. One thing, my eyes have been opened anyway, and I no longer judge so harshly the shiftless and unambitious among my people. I hardly see how a people, who have so much to contend with and so little to hope for, can go on striving and aspiring. But the very fact that they do, breeds in me a respect for them. I now see why so many promising young men, class orators, valedictorians and the like fall by the wayside and are never heard from after commencement day. I now see why the sleeping and dining-car companies are supplied by men with better educations than half the passengers whom they serve. They get tired of swimming always against the tide, as who would not? and are content to drift.

"I know that a good many of my friends would say that I am whining. Well, suppose I am, that's the business of a whipped cur. The dog on top can bark, but the under dog must howl.

"Nothing so breaks a man's spirit as defeat, constant, unaltering, hopeless defeat. That's what I've experienced. I am still studying law in a halfhearted way for I don't know what I am going to do with it when I have been admitted. Diplomas don't draw clients. We have been taught that merit wins. But I have learned that the adages, as well as the books and the formulas were made by and for others than us of the black race.

"They say, too, that our brother Americans sympathize with us, and will help us when we help ourselves. Bah! The only sympathy that I have ever seen on the part of the white man was not for the negro himself, but for some portion of white blood that the colored man had got tangled up in his veins.

"But there, perhaps my disappointment has made me sour, so think no more of what I have said. I am going now to do what I abhor. Going South to try to find a school. It's awful. But I don't want any one to pity me. There are several thousands of us in the same position.

"I am glad you are prospering. You were better equipped than I was with a deal of materialism and a dearth of ideals. Give us a line when you are in good heart.

"Yours, HALLIDAY.

"P.S. — Just as I finished writing I had a note from Judge Featherton offering me the court messengership at five dollars a week. I am twenty-five. The place was held before by a white boy of fifteen. I declined. 'Southward Ho!'"

Davis was not without sympathy as he read his friend's letter in a city some distance away. He had worked in a hotel, saved money enough to start a barber-shop and was prospering. His white customers joked with him and patted him on the back, and he was already known to have political influence. Yes, he sympathized with Bert, but he laughed over the letter and jingled the coins in his pockets.

"Thank heaven," he said, "that I have no ideals to be knocked into a cocked hat. A colored man has no business with ideals — not in *this* nineteenth century!"

JIM'S PROBATION

For so long a time had Jim been known as the hardest sinner on the plantation that no one had tried to reach the heart under his outward shell even in camp-meeting and revival times. Even good old Brother Parker, who was ever looking after the lost and straying sheep, gave him up as beyond recall.

"Dat Jim," he said, "Oomph, de debbil done got his stamp on dat boy, an' dey ain' no use in tryin' to scratch hit off."

"But Parker," said his master, "that's the very sort of man you want to save. Don't you know it's your business as a man of the gospel to call sinners to repentance?"

"Lawd, Mas' Mordaunt," exclaimed the old man, "my v'ice done got hoa'se callin' Jim, too long ergo to talk erbout. You jes' got to let him go 'long, maybe some o' dese days he gwine slip up on de gospel an' fall plum' inter salvation."

Even Mandy, Jim's wife, had attempted to urge the old man to some more active efforts in her husband's behalf. She was a pillar of the church herself, and was woefully disturbed about the condition of Jim's soul. Indeed, it was said that half of the time it was Mandy's prayers and exhortations that drove Jim into the woods with his dog and his axe, or an old gun that he had come into possession of from one of the younger Mordaunts.

Jim was unregenerate. He was a fighter, a hard drinker, fiddled on Sunday, and had been known to go out hunting on that sacred day. So it startled the whole place when Mandy announced one day to a few of her intimate friends that she believed "Jim was under conviction." He had stolen out hunting one Sunday night and in passing through the swamp had gotten himself thoroughly wet and chilled, and this had brought on an attack of acute rheumatism, which Mandy had pointed out to him as a direct judgment of heaven. Jim scoffed at first, but Mandy grew more and more earnest, and finally, with the racking of the pain, he waxed serious and determined to look to the state of his soul as a means to the good of his body.

"Hit do seem," Mandy said, "dat Jim feel de weight o' his sins mos' powahful."

"I reckon hit's de rheumatics," said Dinah.

"Don' mek no diffunce what de inst'ument is," Mandy replied, "hit's de 'sult, hit's de 'sult."

When the news reached Stuart Mordaunt's ears he became intensely interested. Anything that would convert Jim, and make a model Christian of him would be providential on that plantation. It would save the overseers many an hour's worry; his horses, many a secret ride; and the other servants, many a broken head. So he again went down to labor with Parker in the interest of the sinner.

"Is he mou'nin' yit?" said Parker.

"No, not yet, but I think now is a good time to sow the seeds in his mind."

"Oomph," said the old man, "reckon you bettah let Jim alone twell dem sins o' his'n git him to tossin' an' cryin' an' a mou'nin'. Den'll be time enough to strive wid him. I's allus willin' to do my pa't, Mas' Stuart, but w'en hit comes to ol' time sinnahs lak Jim, I believe in layin' off, an' lettin' de sperit do de strivin'."

"But Parker," said his master, "you yourself know that the Bible says that the spirit will not always strive."

"Well, la den, mas', you don' spec' I gwine outdo de sperit."

But Stuart Mordaunt was particularly anxious that Jim's steps might be turned in the right direction. He knew just what a strong hold over their minds the Negroes' own emotional religion had, and he felt that could he once get Jim inside the pale of the church, and put him on guard of his salvation, it would mean the loss of fewer of his shoats and pullets. So he approached the old preacher, and said in a confidential tone.

"Now look here, Parker, I've got a fine lot of that good old tobacco you like so up to the big house, and I'll tell you what I'll do. If you'll just try to work on Jim, and get his feet in the right path, you can come up and take all you want."

"Oom-oomph," said the old man, "dat sho' is monst'ous fine terbaccer, Mas' Stua't."

"Yes, it is, and you shall have all you want of it."

"Well, I'll have a little wisit wid Jim, an' des' see how much he 'fected, an' if dey any stroke to be put in fu' de gospel ahmy, you des' count on me ez a mighty strong wa'ior. Dat boy been layin' heavy on my mind fu' lo, dese many days."

As a result of this agreement, the old man went down to Jim's cabin on a night when that interesting sinner was suffering particularly from his rheumatic pains.

"Well, Jim," the preacher said, "how you come on?"

"Po'ly, po'ly," said Jim, "I des' plum' racked an' 'stracted f'om haid to foot."

"Uh, huh, hit do seem lak to me de Bible don' tell nuffin' else but de trufe."

"What de Bible been sayin' now?" asked Jim suspiciously.

"Des' what it been sayin' all de res' o' de time. 'Yo' sins will fin' you out'"

Jim groaned and turned uneasily in his chair. The old man saw that he had made a point and pursued it.

"Don' you reckon now, Jim, ef you was a bettah man dat you wouldn' suffah so?"

"I do' know, I do' know nuffin' 'bout hit."

"Now des' look at me. I ben a-trompin' erlong in dis low groun' o' sorrer fu' mo' den seventy yeahs, an' I hain't got a ache ner a pain. Nevah had no rheumatics in my life, an' yere you is, a young man, in a mannah o' speakin', all twinged up wid rheumatics. Now what dat p'int to? Hit mean de Lawd tek keer o' dem dat's his'n. Now Jim, you bettah come ovah on de Lawd's side, an' git erway f'om yo' ebil doin's."

Jim groaned again, and lifted his swollen leg with an effort just as Brother Parker said, "Let us pray."

The prayer itself was less effective than the request was just at that time for Jim was so stiff that it made him fairly howl with pain to get down on his knees. The old man's supplication was loud, deep, and diplomatic, and when they arose from their knees there were tears in Jim's eyes, but whether from cramp or contrition it is not safe to say. But a day or two after, the visit bore fruit in the appearance of Jim at meeting where he sat on one of the very last benches, his shoulders hunched, and his head bowed, unmistakable signs of the convicted sinner.

The usual term of mourning passed, and Jim was converted, much to Mandy's joy, and Brother Parker's delight. The old man called early on his master after the meeting, and announced the success of his labors. Stuart Mordaunt himself was no less pleased than the preacher. He shook Parker warmly by the hand, patted him on the shoulder, and called him a "sly old fox." And then he took him to the cupboard, and gave him of his store of good tobacco, enough to last him for months. Something else, too, he must have given him, for the old man came away from the cupboard grinning broadly, and ostentatiously wiping his mouth with the back of his hand.

"Great work you've done, Parker, a great work."

"Yes, yes, Mas'," grinned the old man, "now ef Jim can des' stan' out his p'obation, hit'll be montrous fine."

"His probation!" exclaimed the master.

"Oh yes suh, yes suh, we has all de young convu'ts stan' a p'obation o' six months, fo' we teks 'em reg'lar inter de chu'ch. Now ef Jim will des' stan' strong in de faif —"

"Parker," said Mordaunt, "you're an old wretch, and I've got a mind to take every bit of that tobacco away from you. No. I'll tell you what I'll do."

He went back to the cupboard and got as much again as he had given Parker, and handed it to him saying,

"I think it will be better for all concerned if Jim's probation only lasts two months. Get him into the fold, Parker, get him into the fold!" And he shoved the ancient exhorter out of the door.

It grieved Jim that he could not go 'possum hunting on Sundays any more, but shortly after he got religion, his rheumatism seemed to take a turn for the better and he felt that the result was worth the sacrifice. But as the pain decreased in his legs and arms, the longing for his old wicked pleasures became stronger and stronger upon him though Mandy thought that he was living out the period of his probation in the most exemplary manner, and inwardly rejoiced.

It was two weeks before he was to be regularly admitted to church fellowship. His industrious spouse had decked him out in a bleached cotton shirt in which to attend divine service. In the morning Jim was there. The sermon which Brother Parker preached was powerful, but somehow it failed to reach this new convert. His gaze roved out of the window toward the dark line of the woods beyond, where the frost still glistened on the trees and where he knew the persimmons were hanging ripe. Jim was present at the afternoon service also, for it was a great day; and again, he was preoccupied. He started and clasped his hands together until the bones cracked, when a dog barked somewhere out on the hill. The sun was going down over the tops of the woodland trees, throwing the forest into gloom, as they came out of the log meeting-house. Jim paused and looked lovingly at the scene, and sighed as he turned his steps back toward the cabin.

That night Mandy went to church alone. Jim had disappeared. Nowhere around was his axe, and Spot, his dog, was gone. Mandy looked over toward the woods whose tops were feathered against the frosty sky, and away off, she heard a dog bark.

Brother Parker was feeling his way home from meeting late that night, when all of a sudden, he came upon a man creeping toward the quarters. The man had an axe and a dog, and over his shoulders hung a bag in which the outlines of a 'possum could be seen.

"Hi, oh, Brothah Jim, at it agin?"

Jim did not reply. "Well, des' heish up an' go 'long. We got to mek some 'lowances fu' you young convu'ts. Wen you gwine cook dat 'possum, Brothah Jim?"

"I do' know, Brothah Pahkah. He so po', I 'low I haveter keep him and fatten him fu' awhile."

"Uh, huh! well, so long, Jim."

"So long, Brothah Pahkah." Jim chuckled as he went away. "I 'low I fool dat ol' fox. Wanter come down an' eat up my one little 'possum, do he? huh, uh!"

So that very night Jim scraped his possum, and hung it out-of-doors, and the next day, brown as the forest whence it came, it lay on a great platter on Jim's table. It was a fat possum too. Jim had just whetted his knife, and Mandy had just finished the blessing when the latch was lifted and Brother Parker stepped in.

"Hi, oh, Brothah Jim, I's des' in time."

Jim sat with his mouth open. "Draw up a cheer, Brothah Pahkah," said Mandy. Her husband rose, and put his hand over the possum.

"Wha — wha'd you come hyeah fu'?" he asked.

"I thought I'd des' come in an' tek a bite wid you."

"Ain' gwine tek no bite wid me," said Jim.

"Heish," said Mandy, "wha' kin' o' way is dat to talk to de preachah?"

"Preachah er no preachah, you hyeah what I say," and he took the possum, and put it on the highest shelf.

"Wha's de mattah wid you, Jim; dat's one o' de' 'quiahments o' de chu'ch."

The angry man turned to the preacher.

"Is it one o' de 'quiahments o' de chu'ch dat you eat hyeah ternight?"

"Hit sholy am usual fu' de shepherd to sup wherevah he stop," said Parker suavely.

"Ve'y well, ve'y well," said Jim, "I wants you to know dat I 'specs to stay out o' yo' chu'ch. I's got two weeks mo' p'obation. You tek hit back, an' gin hit to de nex' niggah you ketches wid a 'possum."

Mandy was horrified. The preacher looked longingly at the possum, and took up his hat to go.

There were two disappointed men on the plantation when he told his master the next day the outcome of Jim's probation.

UNCLE SIMON'S SUNDAYS OUT

Mr. Marston sat upon his wide veranda in the cool of the summer Sabbath morning. His hat was off, the soft breeze was playing with his brown hair, and a fragrant cigar was rolled lazily between his lips. He was taking his ease after the fashion of a true gentleman. But his eyes roamed widely, and his glance rested now on the blue-green sweep of the great lawn, again on the bright blades of the growing corn, and anon on the waving fields of tobacco, and he sighed a sigh of ineffable content. The breath had hardly died on his lips when the figure of an old man appeared before him, and, hat in hand, shuffled up the wide steps of the porch.

It was a funny old figure, stooped and so one-sided that the tail of the long and shabby coat he wore dragged on the ground. The face was black and shrewd, and little patches of snow-white hair fringed the shiny pate.

"Good-morning, Uncle Simon," said Mr. Marston, heartily.

"Mornin' Mas' Gawge. How you come on?"

"I'm first-rate. How are you? How are your rheumatics coming on?"

"Oh, my, dey's mos' nigh well. Dey don' trouble me no mo'!"

"Most nigh well, don't trouble you any more?"

"Dat is none to speak of."

"Why, Uncle Simon, who ever heard tell of a man being cured of his aches and pains at your age?"

"I ain' so powahful ol', Mas', I ain' so powahful ol'."

"You're not so powerful old! Why, Uncle Simon, what's taken hold of you? You're eighty if a day."

"Sh — sh, talk dat kin' o' low, Mastah, don' 'spress yo'se'f so loud!" and the old man looked fearfully around as if he feared some one might hear the words.

The master fell back in his seat in utter surprise.

"And, why, I should like to know, may I not speak of your age aloud?"

Uncle Simon showed his two or three remaining teeth in a broad grin as he answered:

"Well, Mastah, I's 'fraid ol' man Time mought hyeah you an' t'ink he done let me run too long." He chuckled, and his master joined him with a merry peal of laughter.

"All right, then, Simon," he said, "I'll try not to give away any of your secrets to old man Time. But isn't your age written down somewhere?"

"I reckon it's in dat ol' Bible yo' pa gin me."

"Oh, let it alone then, even Time won't find it there."

The old man shifted the weight of his body from one leg to the other and stood embarrassedly twirling his ancient hat in his hands. There was evidently something more that he wanted to say. He had not come to exchange commonplaces with his master about age or its ailments.

"Well, what is it now, Uncle Simon?" the master asked, heeding the servant's embarrassment, "I know you've come up to ask or tell me something. Have any of your converts been backsliding, or has Buck been misbehaving again?"

"No, suh, de converts all seem to be stan'in' strong in de faif, and Buck, he actin' right good now."

"Doesn't Lize bring your meals regular, and cook them good?"

"Oh, yes, suh, Lize ain' done nuffin'. Dey ain' nuffin' de mattah at de quahtahs, nuffin' 't'al."

"Well, what on earth then —"

"Hol' on, Mas', hol' on! I done tol' you dey ain' nuffin' de mattah 'mong de people, an' I ain' come to 'plain 'bout nuffin'; but — but — I wants to speak to you 'bout somefin' mighty partic'ler."

"Well, go on, because it will soon be time for you to be getting down to the meeting-house to exhort the hands."

"Dat's jes' what I want to speak 'bout, dat 'zortin'."

"Well, you've been doing it for a good many years now."

"Dat's de very idee, dat's in my haid now. Mas' Gawge, huccume you read me so nigh right?"

"Oh, that's not reading anything, that's just truth. But what do you mean, Uncle Simon, you don't mean to say that you want to resign. Why what would your old wife think if she was living?"

"No, no, Mas' Gawge, I don't ezzactly want to 'sign, but I'd jes' lak to have a few Sundays off."

"A few Sundays off! Well, now, I do believe that you are crazy. What on earth put that into your head?"

"Nuffin', Mas' Gawge, I wants to be away f'om my Sabbaf labohs fu' a little while, dat's all."

"Why, what are the hands going to do for some one to exhort them on Sunday. You know they've got to shout or burst, and it used to be your delight to get them stirred up until all the back field was ringing."

"I do' say dat I ain' gwine try an' do dat some mo', Mastah, min' I do' say dat. But in de mean time I's got somebody else to tek my place, one dat I trained up in de wo'k right undah my own han'. Mebbe he ain' endowed wif de sperrit as I is, all men cain't be gifted de same way, but dey ain't no sputin' he is powahful. Why, he can handle de Scriptures wif bof han's, an' you kin hyeah him prayin' fu' two miles."

"And you want to put this wonder in your place?"

"Yes, suh, fu' a while, anyhow."

"Uncle Simon, aren't you losing your religion?"

"Losin' my u'ligion? Who, me losin' my u'ligion! No, suh."

"Well, aren't you afraid you'll lose it on the Sundays that you spend out of your meeting-house?"

"Now, Mas' Gawge, you a white man, an' you my mastah, an' you got larnin'. But what kin' o' argyment is dat? Is dat good jedgment?"

"Well, now if it isn't, you show me why, you're a logician." There was a twinkle in the eye of George Marston as he spoke.

"No, I ain' no 'gician, Mastah," the old man contended. "But what kin' o' u'ligion you spec' I got anyhow? Hyeah me been sto'in' it up fu' lo, dese many yeahs an' ain' got enough to las' ovah a few Sundays. What kin' o' u'ligion is dat?"

The master laughed, "I believe you've got me there, Uncle Simon; well go along, but see that your flock is well tended."

"Thanky, Mas' Gawge, thanky. I'll put a shepherd in my place dat'll put de food down so low dat de littles' lambs kin enjoy it, but'll mek it strong enough fu' de oldes' ewes." And with a profound bow the old man went down the steps and hobbled away.

As soon as Uncle Simon was out of sight, George Marston threw back his head and gave a long shout of laughter.

"I wonder," he mused, "what crotchet that old darkey has got into his head now. He comes with all the air of a white divine to ask for a vacation. Well, I reckon he deserves it. He had me on the religious argument, too. He's got his grace stored." And another peal of her husband's laughter brought Mrs. Marston from the house.

"George, George, what is the matter. What amuses you so that you forget that this is the Sabbath day?"

"Oh, don't talk to me about Sunday any more, when it comes to the pass that the Reverend Simon Marston wants a vacation. It seems that the cares of his parish have been too pressing upon him and he wishes to be away for some time. He does not say whether he will visit Europe or the Holy Land, however, we shall expect him to come back with much new and interesting material for the edification of his numerous congregation."

"I wish you would tell me what you mean by all this."

Thus adjured, George Marston curbed his amusement long enough to recount to his wife the particulars of his interview with Uncle Simon.

"Well, well, and you carry on so, only because one of the servants wishes his Sundays to himself for awhile? Shame on you!"

"Mrs. Marston," said her husband, solemnly, "you are hopeless — positively, undeniably, hopeless. I do not object to your failing to see the humor in the situation, for you are a woman; but that you should not be curious as to the motives which actuate Uncle Simon, that you should be unmoved by a burning desire to know why this staunch old servant who has for so many years pictured hell each Sunday to his fellow-servants should wish a vacation — that I can neither understand nor forgive."

"Oh, I can see why easily enough, and so could you, if you were not so intent on laughing at everything. The poor old man is tired and wants rest, that's all." And Mrs. Marston turned into the house with a stately step, for she was a proud and dignified lady.

"And that reason satisfies you? Ah, Mrs. Marston, Mrs. Marston, you discredit your sex!" her husband sighed, mockingly after her.

There was perhaps some ground for George Marston's perplexity as to Uncle Simon's intentions. His request for "Sundays off" was so entirely out of the usual order of things. The old man, with the other servants on the plantation had been bequeathed to Marston by his father. Even then, Uncle Simon was an old man, and for many years in the elder Marston's time had been the plantation exhorter. In this position he continued, and as his age increased, did little of anything else. He had a little log house built in a stretch of woods convenient to the quarters, where Sunday after Sunday he held forth to as many of the hands as could be encouraged to attend.

With time, the importance of his situation grew upon him. He would have thought as soon of giving up his life as his pulpit to any one else. He was never absent a single meeting day in all that time. Sunday after Sunday he was in his place expounding his doctrine. He had grown officious, too, and if any of his congregation were away from service, Monday morning found him early at their cabins to find out the reason why.

After a life, then, of such punctilious rigidity, it is no wonder that his master could not accept Mrs. Marston's simple excuse for Uncle Simon's dereliction, "that the old man needed rest." For the time being, the good lady might have her way, as all good ladies should, but as for him, he chose to watch and wait and speculate.

Mrs. Marston, however, as well as her husband, was destined to hear more that day of Uncle Simon's strange move, for there was one other person on the place who was not satisfied with Uncle Simon's explanation of his conduct, and yet could not as easily as the mistress formulate an opinion of her own. This was Lize, who did about the quarters and cooked the meals of the older servants who were no longer in active service.

It was just at the dinner hour that she came hurrying up to the "big house," and with the freedom of an old and privileged retainer went directly to the dining-room.

"Look hyeah, Mis' M'ree," she exclaimed, without the formality of prefacing her remarks, "I wants to know whut's de mattah wif Brothah Simon — what mek him ac' de way he do?"

"Why, I do not know, Eliza, what has Uncle Simon been doing?"

"Why, some o' you all mus' know, lessn' he couldn' 'a' done hit. Ain' he ax you nuffin', Marse Gawge?"

"Yes, he did have some talk with me."

"Some talk! I reckon he did have some talk wif somebody!"

"Tell us, Lize," Mr. Marston said, "what has Uncle Simon done?"

"He done brung somebody else, dat young Merrit darky, to oc'py his pu'pit. He in'juce him, an' 'en he say dat he gwine be absent a few Sundays, an' 'en he tek hissef off, outen de chu'ch, widout even waitin' fu' de sehmont."

"Well, didn't you have a good sermon?"

"It mought 'a' been a good sehmont, but dat ain' whut I ax you. I want to know whut de mattah wif Brothah Simon."

"Why, he told me that the man he put over you was one of the most powerful kind, warranted to make you shout until the last bench was turned over."

"Oh, some o' dem, dey shouted enough, dey shouted dey fill. But dat ain' whut I's drivin' at yit. Whut I wan' 'o know, whut mek Brothah Simon do dat?"

"Well, I'll tell you, Lize," Marston began, but his wife cut him off.

"Now, George," she said, "you shall not trifle with Eliza in that manner." Then turning to the old servant, she said: "Eliza, it means nothing. Do not trouble yourself about it. You know Uncle Simon is old; he has been exhorting for you now for many years, and he needs a little rest these Sundays. It is getting toward midsummer, and it is warm and wearing work to preach as Uncle Simon does."

Lize stood still, with an incredulous and unsatisfied look on her face. After a while she said, dubiously shaking her head:

"Huh uh! Miss M'ree, dat may 'splain t'ings to you, but hit ain' mek 'em light to me yit."

"Now, Mrs. Marston" — began her husband, chuckling.

"Hush, I tell you, George. It's really just as I tell you, Eliza, the old man is tired and needs rest!"

Again the old woman shook her head, "Huh uh," she said, "ef you'd' a' seen him gwine lickety split outen de meetin'-house you wouldn' a thought he was so tiahed."

Marston laughed loud and long at this. "Well, Mrs. Marston," he bantered, "even Lize is showing a keener perception of the fitness of things than you."

"There are some things I can afford to be excelled in by my husband and my servants. For my part, I have no suspicion of Uncle Simon, and no concern about him either one way or the other."

"'Scuse me, Miss M'ree," said Lize, "I didn' mean no ha'm to you, but I ain' a trustin' ol' Brothah Simon, I tell you."

"I'm not blaming you, Eliza; you are sensible as far as you know."

"Ahem," said Mr. Marston.

Eliza went out mumbling to herself, and Mr. Marston confined his attentions to his dinner; he chuckled just once, but Mrs. Marston met his levity with something like a sniff.

On the first two Sundays that Uncle Simon was away from his congregation nothing was known about his whereabouts. On the third Sunday he was reported to have been seen making his way toward the west plantation. Now what did this old man want there? The west plantation, so called, was a part of the Marston domain, but the land there was worked by a number of slaves which Mrs. Marston had brought with her from Louisiana, where she had given up her father's gorgeous home on the Bayou Lafourche, together with her proud name of Marie St. Pierre for George Marston's love. There had been so many bickerings between the Marston servants and the contingent from Louisiana that the two sets had been separated, the old remaining on the east side and the new ones going to the west. So, to those who had been born on the soil the name of the west plantation became a reproach. It was a synonym for all that was worldly, wicked and unregenerate. The east plantation did not visit with the west. The east gave a dance, the west did not attend. The Marstons and St. Pierres in black did not intermarry. If a Marston died, a St. Pierre did not sit up with him. And so the division had kept up for years.

It was hardly to be believed then that Uncle Simon Marston, the very patriarch of the Marston flock, was visiting over the border. But on another Sunday he was seen to go straight to the west plantation.

At her first opportunity Lize accosted him: —

"Look a-hyeah, Brothah Simon, whut's dis I been hyeahin' 'bout you, huh?"

"Well, sis' Lize, I reckon you'll have to tell me dat yo' se'f, 'case I do' know. Whut you been hyeahin'?"

"Brothah Simon, you's a ol' man, you's ol'."

"Well, sis' Lize, dah was Methusalem."

"I ain' jokin', Brothah Simon, I ain' jokin', I's a talkin' right straight-fo'wa'd. Yo' conduc' don' look right. Hit ain' becomin' to you as de shep-herd of a flock."

"But whut I been doin', sistah, whut I been doin'?"

"You know."

"I reckon I do, but I wan' see whethah you does er not."

"You been gwine ovah to de wes' plantation, dat's whut you been doin'. You can' 'ny dat, you's been seed!"

"I do' wan' 'ny it. Is dat all?"

"Is dat all!" Lize stood aghast. Then she said slowly and wonderingly, "Brothah Simon, is you losin' yo' senses er yo' grace?"

"I ain' losin' one ner 'tothah, but I do' see no ha'm in gwine ovah to de wes' plantation."

"You do' see no ha'm in gwine ovah to de wes' plantation! You stan' hyeah in sight o' Gawd an' say dat?"

"Don't git so 'cited, sis' Lize, you mus' membah dat dey's souls on de wes' plantation, jes' same as dey is on de eas'."

"Yes, an' dey's souls in hell, too," the old woman fired back.

"Cose dey is, but dey's already damned; but dey's souls on de wes' planta-tion to be saved."

"Oomph, uh, uh, uh!" grunted Lize.

"You done called me de shepherd, ain't you, sistah? Well, sayin' I is, when dey's little lambs out in de col' an' dey ain' got sense 'nough to come in, er dey do' know de way, whut do de shepherd do? Why, he go out, an' he hunt up de po' shiverin', bleatin' lambs and brings 'em into de fol'. Don't you bothah 'bout de wes' plantation, sis' Lize." And Uncle Simon hobbled off down the road with surprising alacrity, leaving his interlocutor standing with mouth and eyes wide open.

"Well, I nevah!" she exclaimed when she could get her lips together, "I do believe de day of jedgmen' is at han'."

Of course this conversation was duly reported to the master and mis-tress, and called forth some strictures from Mrs. Marston on Lize's attempted interference with the old man's good work.

"You ought to be ashamed of yourself, Eliza, that you ought. After the estrangement of all this time if Uncle Simon can effect a reconciliation between the west and the east plantations, you ought not to lay a straw in his way. I am sure there is more of a real Christian spirit in that than in shouting and singing for hours, and then coming out with your heart full of malice. You need not laugh, Mr. Marston, you need not laugh at all. I am very much in earnest, and I do hope that Uncle Simon will continue his ministrations on the other side. If he wants to, he can have a room built in which to lead their worship."

"But you do' want him to leave us altogethah?"

"If you do not care to share your meeting-house with them, they can have one of their own."

"But, look hyeah, Missy, dem Lousiany people, dey bad — an' dey hoodoo folks, an' dey Cath'lics —"

"Eliza!"

"'Scuse me, Missy, chile, bless yo' hea't, you know I do' mean no ha'm to you. But somehow I do' feel right in my hea't 'bout Brothah Simon."

"Never mind, Eliza, it is only evil that needs to be watched, the good will take care of itself."

It was not one, nor two, nor three Sundays that Brother Simon was away from his congregation, but six passed before he was there again. He was seen to be very busy tinkering around during the week, and then one Sunday he appeared suddenly in his pulpit. The church nodded and smiled a welcome to him. There was no change in him. If anything he was more fiery than ever. But, there was a change. Lize, who was news-gatherer and carrier extraordinary, bore the tidings to her owners. She burst into the big house with the cry of "Whut I tell you! Whut I tell you!"

"Well, what now," exclaimed both Mr. and Mrs. Marston.

"Didn' I tell you ol' Simon was up to some'p'n?"

"Out with it," exclaimed her master, "out with it, I knew he was up to something, too."

"George, try to remember who you are."

"Brothah Simon come in chu'ch dis mo'nin' an' he 'scended up de pulpit —"

"Well, what of that, are you not glad he is back?"

"Hol' on, lemme tell you — he 'scended up de pu'pit, an' 'menced his disco'se. Well, he hadn't no sooner got sta'ted when in walked one o' dem brazen Lousiany wenches —"

"Eliza!"

"Hol' on, Miss M'ree, she walked in lak she owned de place, an' flopped huhse'f down on de front seat."

"Well, what if she did," burst in Mrs. Marston, "she had a right. I want you to understand, you and the rest of your kind, that that meeting-house is for any of the hands that care to attend it. The woman did right. I hope she'll come again."

"I hadn' got done yit, Missy. Jes' ez soon ez de sehmont was ovah, whut mus' Brothah Simon, de 'zortah, min' you, whut mus' he do but come hoppin' down f'om de pu'pit, an' beau dat wench home! 'Scorted huh clah 'crost de plantation befo' evahbody's face. Now whut you call dat?"

"I call it politeness, that is what I call it. What are you laughing at, Mr. Marston? I have no doubt that the old man was merely trying to set an example of courtesy to some of the younger men, or to protect the woman from the insults that the other members of the congregation would heap upon her. Mr. Marston, I do wish you would keep your face serious. There is nothing to laugh at in this matter. A worthy old man tries to do a worthy work, his fellow-servants cavil at him, and his master, who should encourage him, laughs at him for his pains."

"I assure you, my dear, I'm not laughing at Uncle Simon."

"Then at me, perhaps; that is infinitely better."

"And not at you, either; I'm amused at the situation."

"Well, Manette ca'ied him off dis mo'nin'," resumed Eliza.

"Manette!" exclaimed Mrs. Marston.

"It was Manette he was a beauin'. Evahbody say he likin' huh moughty well, an' dat he look at huh all th'oo preachin'."

"Oh my! Manette's one of the nicest girls I brought from St. Pierre. I hope — oh, but then she is a young woman, she would not think of being foolish over an old man."

"I do' know, Miss M'ree. De ol' men is de wuss kin'. De young oomans knows how to tek de young mans, 'case dey de same age, an' dey been lu'nin' dey tricks right along wif dem'; but de ol' men, dey got sich a long sta't ahaid, dey been lu'nin' so long. Ef I had a darter, I wouldn' be afeard to let huh tek keer o' huhse'f wif a young man, but ef a ol' man come a cou'tin' huh, I'd keep my own two eyes open."

"Eliza, you're a philosopher," said Mr. Marston. "You're one of the few reasoners of your sex."

"It is all nonsense," said his wife. "Why Uncle Simon is old enough to be Manette's grandfather."

"Love laughs at years."

"And you laugh at everything."

"That's the difference between love and me, my dear Mrs. Marston."

"Do not pay any attention to your master, Eliza, and do not be so suspicious of every one. It is all right. Uncle Simon had Manette over, because he thought the service would do her good."

"Yes'm, I 'low she's one o' de young lambs dat he gone out in de col' to fotch in. Well, he tek'n' moughty good keer o' dat lamb.'"

Mrs. Marston was compelled to laugh in spite of herself. But when Eliza was gone, she turned to her husband, and said:

"George, dear, do you really think there is anything in it?"

"I thoroughly agree with you, Mrs. Marston, in the opinion that Uncle Simon needed rest, and I may add on my own behalf, recreation."

"Pshaw! I do not believe it."

All doubts, however, were soon dispelled. The afternoon sun drove Mr. Marston to the back veranda where he was sitting when Uncle Simon again approached and greeted him.

"Well, Uncle Simon, I hear that you're back in your pulpit again?"

"Yes, suh, I's done 'sumed my labohs in de Mastah's vineya'd.'"

"Have you had a good rest of it?"

"Well, I ain' ezzackly been restin'," said the aged man, scratching his head. "I's been pu'su'in' othah 'ployments."

"Oh, yes, but change of work is rest. And how's the rheumatism, now, any better?"

"Bettah? Why, Mawse Gawge, I ain' got a smidgeon of hit. I's jes' limpin' a leetle bit on 'count o' habit."

"Well, it's good if one can get well, even if his days are nearly spent."

"Heish, Mas' Gawge. I ain' t'inkin' 'bout dyin'."

"Aren't you ready yet, in all these years?"

"I hope I's ready, but I hope to be spaihed a good many yeahs yit."

"To do good, I suppose?"

"Yes, suh; yes, suh. Fac' is, Mawse Gawge, I jes' hop up to ax you some'p'n."

"Well, here I am."

"I want to ax you — I want to ax you — er — er — I want —"

"Oh, speak out. I haven't time to be bothering here all day."

"Well, you know, Mawse Gawge, some o' us ain' nigh ez ol' ez dey looks."

"That's true. A person, now, would take you for ninety, and to my positive knowledge, you're not more than eighty-five."

"Oh, Lawd. Mastah, do heish."

"I'm not flattering you, that's the truth."

"Well, now, Mawse Gawge, couldn' you mek me' look lak eighty-fo', an' be a little youngah?"

"Why, what do you want to be younger for?"

"You see, hit's jes' lak dis, Mawse Gawge. I come up hyeah to ax you — I want — dat is — me an' Manette, we wants to git ma'ied."

"Get married!" thundered Marston. "What you, you old scarecrow, with one foot in the grave!"

"Heish, Mastah, 'buse me kin' o' low. Don't th'ow yo' words 'roun' so keerless."

"This is what you wanted your Sundays off for, to go sparking around — you an exhorter, too."

"But I's been missin' my po' ol' wife so much hyeah lately."

"You've been missing her, oh, yes, and so you want to get a woman young enough to be your granddaughter to fill her place."

"Well, Mas' Gawge, you know, ef I is ol' an' feeble, ez you say, I need a strong young han' to he'p me down de hill, an' ef Manette don' min' spa'in' a few mont's er yeahs —"

"That'll do, I'll see what your mistress says. Come back in an hour."

A little touched, and a good deal amused, Marston went to see his wife. He kept his face straight as he addressed her. "Mrs. Marston, Manette's hand has been proposed for."

"George!"

"The Rev. Simon Marston has this moment come and solemnly laid his heart at my feet as proxy for Manette."

"He shall not have her, he shall not have her!" exclaimed the lady, rising angrily.

"But remember, Mrs. Marston, it will keep her coming to meeting."

"I do not care; he is an old hypocrite, that is what he is."

"Think, too, of what a noble work he is doing. It brings about a reconciliation between the east and west plantations, for which we have been hoping for years. You really oughtn't to lay a straw in his way."

"He's a sneaking, insidious, old scoundrel."

"Such poor encouragement from his mistress for a worthy old man, who only needs rest!"

"George!" cried Mrs. Marston, and she sank down in tears, which turned to convulsive laughter as her husband put his arm about her and whispered, "He is showing the true Christian spirit. Don't you think we'd better call Manette and see if she consents? She is one of his lambs, you know."

"Oh, George, George, do as you please. If the horrid girl consents, I wash my hands of the whole affair."

"You know these old men have been learning such a long while."

By this time Mrs. Marston was as much amused as her husband. Manette was accordingly called and questioned. The information was elicited from her that she loved "Brothah Simon" and wished to marry him.

"'Love laughs at age,'" quoted Mr. Marston again when the girl had been dismissed. Mrs. Marston was laughingly angry, but speechless for a moment. Finally she said: "Well, Manette seems willing, so there is nothing for us to do but to consent, although, mind you, I do not approve of this foolish marriage, do you hear?"

After a while the old man returned for his verdict. He took it calmly. He had expected it. The disparity in the years of him and his betrothed did not seem to strike his consciousness at all. He only grinned.

"Now look here, Uncle Simon," said his master, "I want you to tell me how you, an old, bad-looking, half-dead darky won that likely young girl."

The old man closed one eye and smiled.

"Mastah, I don' b'lieve you looks erroun' you," he said. "Now, 'mongst white folks, you knows a preachah 'mongst de ladies is mos' nigh i'sistible, but 'mongst col'ed dey ain't no pos'ble way to git erroun' de gospel man w'en he go ahuntin' fu' anything."

MR. CORNELIUS JOHNSON, OFFICE-SEEKER

It was a beautiful day in balmy May and the sun shone pleasantly on Mr. Cornelius Johnson's very spruce Prince Albert suit of grey as he alighted from the train in Washington. He cast his eyes about him, and then gave a sigh of relief and satisfaction as he took his bag from the porter and started for the gate. As he went along, he looked with splendid complacency upon the less fortunate mortals who were streaming out of the day coaches. It was a Pullman sleeper on which he had come in. Out on the pavement he hailed a cab, and giving the driver the address of a hotel, stepped in and was rolled away. Be it said that he had cautiously inquired about the hotel first and found that he could be accommodated there.

As he leaned back in the vehicle and allowed his eyes to roam over the streets, there was an air of distinct prosperity about him. It was in evidence from the tips of his ample patent-leather shoes to the crown of the soft felt hat that sat rakishly upon his head. His entrance into Washington had been long premeditated, and he had got himself up accordingly.

It was not such an imposing structure as he had fondly imagined, before which the cab stopped and set Mr. Johnson down. But then he reflected that it was about the only house where he could find accommodation at all, and he was content. In Alabama one learns to be philosophical. It is good to be philosophical in a place where the proprietor of a café fumbles vaguely around in the region of his hip pocket and insinuates that he doesn't want one's custom. But the visitor's ardor was not cooled for all that. He signed the register with a flourish, and bestowed a liberal fee upon the shabby boy who carried his bag to his room.

"Look here, boy," he said, "I am expecting some callers soon. If they come, just send them right up to my room. You take good care of me and look sharp when I ring and you'll not lose anything."

Mr. Cornelius Johnson always spoke in a large and important tone. He said the simplest thing with an air so impressive as to give it the character of a pronouncement. Indeed, his voice naturally was round, mellifluous and persuasive. He carried himself always as if he were passing under his own triumphal arch. Perhaps, more than anything else, it was these qualities of speech and bearing that had made him invaluable on the stump in the recent campaign in Alabama. Whatever it was that held the secret of his power, the man and principles for which he had labored triumphed, and he had come to Washington to reap his reward. He had been assured that his services would not be forgotten, and it was no intention of his that they should be.

After a while he left his room and went out, returning later with several gentlemen from the South and a Washington man. There is some freemasonry among these office-seekers in Washington that throws them inevitably together. The men with whom he returned were such characters as the press would designate as "old wheel-horses" or "pillars of the party." They all adjourned to the bar, where they had something at their host's expense. Then they repaired to his room, whence for the ensuing two hours the bell and the bell-boy were kept briskly going.

The gentleman from Alabama was in his glory. His gestures as he held forth were those of a gracious and condescending prince. It was his first visit to the city, and he said to the Washington man: "I tell you, sir, you've got a mighty fine town here. Of course, there's no opportunity for anything like local pride, because it's the outsiders, or the whole country, rather, that makes it what it is, but that's nothing. It's a fine town, and I'm right sorry that I can't stay longer."

"How long do you expect to be with us, Professor?" inquired Col. Mason, the horse who had bent his force to the party wheel in the Georgia ruts.

"Oh, about ten days, I reckon, at the furthest. I want to spend some time sight-seeing. I'll drop in on the Congressman from my district tomorrow, and call a little later on the President."

"Uh, huh!" said Col. Mason. He had been in the city for some time.

"Yes, sir, I want to get through with my little matter and get back home. I'm not asking for much, and I don't anticipate any trouble in securing what I desire. You see, it's just like this, there's no way for them to refuse us. And if any one deserves the good things at the hands of the administration, who more than we old campaigners, who have been helping the party through its fights from the time that we had our first votes?"

"Who, indeed?" said the Washington man.

"I tell you, gentlemen, the administration is no fool. It knows that we hold the colored vote down there in our vest pockets and it ain't going to turn us down."

"No, of course not, but sometimes there are delays —"

"Delays, to be sure, where a man doesn't know how to go about the matter. The thing to do, is to go right to the centre of authority at once. Don't you see?"

"Certainly, certainly," chorused the other gentlemen.

Before going, the Washington man suggested that the newcomer join them that evening and see something of society at the capital. "You know," he said, "that outside of New Orleans, Washington is the only town in the country that has any colored society to speak of, and I feel that you distinguished men from different sections of the country owe it to our people that they should be allowed to see you. It would be an inspiration to them."

So the matter was settled, and promptly at 8:30 o'clock Mr. Cornelius Johnson joined his friends at the door of his hotel. The grey Prince Albert was scrupulously buttoned about his form, and a shiny top hat replaced the felt of the afternoon. Thus clad, he went forth into society, where he need be followed only long enough to note the magnificence of his manners and the enthusiasm of his reception when he was introduced as Prof. Cornelius Johnson, of Alabama, in a tone which insinuated that he was the only really great man his state had produced.

It might also be stated as an effect of this excursion into Vanity Fair, that when he woke the next morning he was in some doubt as to whether he should visit his Congressman or send for that individual to call upon him. He had felt the subtle flattery of attention from that section of colored society which imitates — only imitates, it is true, but better than any other, copies — the kindnesses and cruelties, the niceties and deceits, of its white prototype. And for the time, like a man in a fog, he had lost his sense of proportion and perspective. But habit finally triumphed, and he called upon the Congressman, only to be met by an under-secretary who told him that his superior was too busy to see him that morning.

"But —"

"Too busy," repeated the secretary.

Mr. Johnson drew himself up and said: "Tell Congressman Barker that Mr. Johnson, Mr. Cornelius Johnson, of Alabama, desires to see him. I think he will see me."

"Well, I can take your message," said the clerk, doggedly, "but I tell you now it won't do you any good. He won't see any one."

But, in a few moments an inner door opened, and the young man came out followed by the desired one. Mr. Johnson couldn't resist the temptation to let his eyes rest on the underling in a momentary glance of triumph as Congressman Barker hurried up to him, saying: "Why, why, Cornelius, how'do? how'do? Ah, you came about that little matter, didn't you? Well, well, I haven't forgotten you; I haven't forgotten you."

The colored man opened his mouth to speak, but the other checked him and went on: "I'm sorry, but I'm in a great hurry now. I'm compelled to leave town today, much against my will, but I shall be back in a week; come around and see me then. Always glad to see you, you know. Sorry I'm so busy now; good-morning, good-morning."

Mr. Johnson allowed himself to be guided politely, but decidedly, to the door. The triumph died out of his face as the reluctant good-morning fell from his lips. As he walked away, he tried to look upon the matter philosophically. He tried to reason with himself — to prove to his own consciousness that the Congressman was very busy and could not give the time that morning. He wanted to make himself believe that he had not been slighted or treated with scant ceremony. But, try as he would, he continued to feel an obstinate, nasty sting that would not let him rest, nor forget his reception. His pride was hurt. The thought came to him to go at once to the President, but he had experience enough to know that such a visit would be vain until he had seen the dispenser of patronage for his district. Thus, there was nothing for him to do but to wait the necessary week. A whole week! His brow knitted as he thought of it.

In the course of these cogitations, his walk brought him to his hotel, where he found his friends of the night before awaiting him. He tried to put on a cheerful face. But his disappointment and humiliation showed through his smile, as the hollows and bones through the skin of a cadaver.

"Well, what luck?" asked Col. Mason, cheerfully.

"Are we to congratulate you?" put in Mr. Perry.

"Not yet, not yet, gentlemen. I have not seen the President yet. The fact is — ahem — my Congressman is out of town."

He was not used to evasions of this kind, and he stammered slightly and his yellow face turned brick-red with shame.

"It is most annoying," he went on, "most annoying. Mr. Barker won't be back for a week, and I don't want to call on the President until I have had a talk with him."

"Certainly not," said Col. Mason, blandly. "There will be delays." This was not his first pilgrimage to Mecca.

Mr. Johnson looked at him gratefully. "Oh, yes; of course, delays," he assented; "most natural. Have something."

At the end of the appointed time, the office-seeker went again to see the Congressman. This time he was admitted without question, and got the chance to state his wants. But somehow, there seemed to be innumerable obstacles in the way. There were certain other men whose wishes had to be consulted; the leader of one of the party factions, who, for the sake of harmony, had to be appeased. Of course, Mr. Johnson's worth was fully recognized, and he would be rewarded according to his deserts. His interests would be looked after. He should drop in again in a day or two. It took time, of course, it took time.

Mr. Johnson left the office unnerved by his disappointment. He had thought it would be easy to come up to Washington, claim and get what he wanted, and, after a glance at the town, hurry back to his home and his honors. It had all seemed so easy — before election; but now —

A vague doubt began to creep into his mind that turned him sick at heart. He knew how they had treated Davis, of Louisiana. He had heard how they had once kept Brotherton, of Texas — a man who had spent all his life in the service of his party — waiting clear through a whole administration, at the end of which the opposite party had come into power. All the stories of disappointment and disaster that he had ever heard came back to him, and he began to wonder if some one of these things was going to happen to him.

Every other day for the next two weeks, he called upon Barker, but always with the same result. Nothing was clear yet, until one day the bland legislator told him that considerations of expediency had compelled them to give the place he was asking for to another man.

"But what am I to do?" asked the helpless man.

"Oh, you just bide your time. I'll look out for you. Never fear."

Until now, Johnson had ignored the gentle hints of his friend, Col. Mason, about a boarding-house being more convenient than a hotel. Now, he asked him if there was a room vacant where he was staying, and finding that there was, he had his things moved thither at once. He felt the change keenly, and although no one really paid any attention to it, he believed that all Washington must have seen it, and hailed it as the first step in his degradation.

For a while the two together made occasional excursions to a glittering palace down the street, but when the money had grown lower and lower Col. Mason had the knack of bringing "a little something" to their rooms without a loss of dignity. In fact, it was in these hours with the old man, over a pipe and a bit of something, that Johnson was most nearly cheerful. Hitch after hitch had occurred in his plans, and day after day he had come home unsuccessful and discouraged. The crowning disappointment, though, came when, after a long session that lasted even up into the hot days of summer, Congress adjourned and his one hope went away. Johnson saw him just before his departure, and listened ruefully as he said: "I tell you, Cornelius, now, you'd better go on home, get back to your business and come again next year. The clouds of battle will be somewhat dispelled by then and we can see clearer what to do. It was too early this year. We were too near the fight still, and there were party wounds to be bound up and little factional sores that had to be healed. But next year, Cornelius, next year we'll see what we can do for you."

His constituent did not tell him that even if his pride would let him go back home a disappointed applicant, he had not the means wherewith to go. He did not tell him that he was trying to keep up appearances and hide the truth from his wife, who, with their two children, waited and hoped for him at home.

When he went home that night, Col. Mason saw instantly that things had gone wrong with him. But here the tact and delicacy of the old politician came uppermost and, without trying to draw his story from him — for he already divined the situation too well — he sat for a long time telling the younger man stories of the ups and downs of men whom he had known in his long and active life.

They were stories of hardship, deprivation and discouragement. But the old man told them ever with the touch of cheeriness and the note of humor that took away the ghastly hopelessness of some of the pictures. He told them with such feeling and sympathy that Johnson was moved to frankness and told him his own pitiful tale.

Now that he had some one to whom he could open his heart, Johnson himself was no less willing to look the matter in the face, and even during the long summer days, when he had begun to live upon his wardrobe, piece by piece, he still kept up; although some of his pomposity went, along with the Prince Albert coat and the shiny hat. He now wore a shiny coat, and less showy head-gear. For a couple of weeks, too, he disappeared, and as he returned with some money, it was fair to presume that he had been at work somewhere, but he could not stay away from the city long.

It was nearing the middle of autumn when Col. Mason came home to their rooms one day to find his colleague more disheartened and depressed than he had ever seen him before. He was lying with his head upon his folded arm, and when he looked up there were traces of tears upon his face.

"Why, why, what's the matter now?" asked the old man. "No bad news, I hope."

"Nothing worse than I should have expected," was the choking answer. "It's a letter from my wife. She's sick and one of the babies is down, but" — his voice broke — "she tells me to stay and fight it out. My God, Mason, I could stand it if she whined or accused me or begged me to come home, but her patient, long-suffering bravery breaks me all up."

Col. Mason stood up and folded his arms across his big chest. "She's a brave little woman," he said, gravely. "I wish her husband was as brave a man." Johnson raised his head and arms from the table where they were sprawled, as the old man went on: "The hard conditions of life in our race have taught our women a patience and fortitude which the women of no other race have ever displayed. They have taught the men less, and I am sorry, very sorry. The thing, that as much as anything else, made the blacks such excellent soldiers in the civil war was their patient endurance of hardship. The softer education of more prosperous days seems to have weakened this quality. The man who quails or weakens in this fight of ours against adverse circumstances would have quailed before — no, he would have run from an enemy on the field."

"Why, Mason, your mood inspires me. I feel as if I could go forth to battle cheerfully." For the moment, Johnson's old pomposity had returned to him, but in the next, a wave of despondency bore it down. "But that's just it; a body feels as if he could fight if he only had something to fight. But here you strike out and hit — nothing. It's only a contest with time. It's waiting — waiting — waiting!"

"In this case, waiting is fighting."

"Well, even that granted, it matters not how grand his cause, the soldier needs his rations."

"Forage," shot forth the answer like a command.

"Ah, Mason, that's well enough in good country; but the army of office-seekers has devastated Washington. It has left a track as bare as lay behind Sherman's troopers." Johnson rose more cheerfully. "I'm going to the telegraph office," he said as he went out.

A few days after this, he was again in the best of spirits, for there was money in his pocket.

"What have you been doing?" asked Mr. Toliver.

His friend laughed like a boy. "Something very imprudent, I'm sure you will say. I've mortgaged my little place down home. It did not bring much, but I had to have money for the wife and the children, and to keep me until Congress assembles; then I believe that everything will be all right."

Col. Mason's brow clouded and he sighed.

On the reassembling of the two Houses, Congressman Barker was one of the first men in his seat. Mr. Cornelius Johnson went to see him soon.

"What, you here already, Cornelius?" asked the legislator.

"I haven't been away," was the answer.

"Well, you've got the hang-on, and that's what an officer-seeker needs. Well, I'll attend to your matter among the very first. I'll visit the President in a day or two."

The listener's heart throbbed hard. After all his waiting, triumph was his at last.

He went home walking on air, and Col. Mason rejoiced with him. In a few days came word from Barker: "Your appointment was sent in today. I'll rush it through on the other side. Come up tomorrow afternoon."

Cornelius and Mr. Toliver hugged each other.

"It came just in time," said the younger man; "the last of my money was about gone, and I should have had to begin paying off that mortgage with no prospect of ever doing it."

The two had suffered together, and it was fitting that they should be together to receive the news of the long-desired happiness; so arm in arm they sauntered down to the Congressman's office about five o'clock the next afternoon. In honor of the occasion, Mr. Johnson had spent his last dollar in redeeming the grey Prince Albert and the shiny hat. A smile flashed across Barker's face as he noted the change.

"Well, Cornelius," he said, "I'm glad to see you still prosperous-looking, for there were some alleged irregularities in your methods down in Alabama, and the Senate has refused to confirm you. I did all I could for you, but —"

The rest of the sentence was lost, as Col. Mason's arms received his friend's fainting form.

"Poor devil!" said the Congressman. "I should have broken it more gently."

Somehow Col. Mason got him home and to bed, where for nine weeks he lay wasting under a complete nervous give-down. The little wife and the children came up to nurse him, and the woman's ready industry helped him to such creature comforts as his sickness demanded. Never once did she murmur; never once did her faith in him waver. And when he was well enough to be moved back, it was money that she had earned, increased by what Col. Mason, in his generosity of spirit, took from his own narrow means, that paid their second-class fare back to the South.

During the fever-fits of his illness, the wasted politician first begged piteously that they would not send him home unplaced, and then he would break out in the most extravagant and pompous boasts about his position, his Congressman and his influence. When he came to himself, he was silent, morose, and bitter. Only once did he melt. It was when he held Col. Mason's hand and bade him good-bye. Then the tears came into his eyes, and what he would have said was lost among his broken words.

As he stood upon the platform of the car as it moved out, and gazed at the white dome and feathery spires of the city, growing into grey indefiniteness, he ground his teeth, and raising his spent hand, shook it at the receding view. "Damn you! damn you!" he cried. "Damn your deceit, your fair cruelties; damn you, you hard, white liar!"

AN OLD-TIME CHRISTMAS

When the holidays came round the thoughts of 'Liza Ann Lewis always turned to the good times that she used to have at home when, following the precedent of anti-bellum days, Christmas lasted all the week and good cheer held sway. She remembered with regret the gifts that were given, the songs that were sung to the tinkling of the banjo and the dances with which they beguiled the night hours. And the eating! Could she forget it? The great turkey, with the fat literally bursting from him; the yellow yam melting into deliciousness in the mouth; or in some more fortunate season, even the juicy 'possum grinning in brown and greasy death from the great platter.

In the ten years she had lived in New York, she had known no such feast-day. Food was strangely dear in the Metropolis, and then there was always the weekly rental of the poor room to be paid. But she had kept the memory of the old times green in her heart, and ever turned to it with the fondness of one for something irretrievably lost.

That is how Jimmy came to know about it. Jimmy was thirteen and small for his age, and he could not remember any such times as his mother told him about. Although he said with great pride to his partner and rival, Blinky Scott, "Chee, Blink, you ought to hear my ol' lady talk about de times dey have down w'ere we come from at Christmas; N'Yoick ain't in it wid dem, you kin jist bet." And Blinky, who was a New Yorker clear through with a New Yorker's contempt for anything outside of the city, had promptly replied with a downward spreading of his right hand, "Aw fu'git it!"

Jimmy felt a little crest-fallen for a minute, but he lifted himself in his own estimation by threatening to "do" Blinky and the cloud rolled by.

'Liza Ann knew that Jimmy couldn't ever understand what she meant by an old-time Christmas unless she could show him by some faint approach to its merrymaking, and it had been the dream of her life to do this. But every year she had failed, until now she was a little ahead.

Her plan was too good to keep, and when Jimmy went out that Christmas eve morning to sell his papers, she had disclosed it to him and bade him hurry home as soon as he was done, for they were to have a real old-time Christmas.

Jimmy exhibited as much pleasure as he deemed consistent with his dignity and promised to be back early to add his earnings to the fund for celebration.

When he was gone, 'Liza Ann counted over her savings lovingly and dreamed of what she would buy her boy, and what she would have for dinner on the next day. Then a voice, a colored man's voice, she knew, floated up to her. Some one in the alley below her window was singing "The Old Folks at Home."

> *"All up an' down the whole creation,*
> *Sadly I roam,*
> *Still longing for the old plantation,*
> *An' for the old folks at home."*

She leaned out of the window and listened and when the song had ceased and she drew her head in again, there were tears in her eyes — the tears of memory and longing. But she crushed them away, and laughed tremulously to herself as she said, "What a reg'lar ol' fool I'm a-gittin' to be." Then she went out into the cold, snow-covered streets, for she had work to do that day that would add a mite to her little Christmas store.

Down in the street, Jimmy was calling out the morning papers and racing with Blinky Scott for prospective customers; these were only transients, of course, for each had his regular buyers whose preferences were scrupulously respected by both in agreement with a strange silent compact.

The electric cars went clanging to and fro, the streets were full of shoppers with bundles and bunches of holly, and all the sights and sounds were pregnant with the message of the joyous time. People were full of the holiday spirit. The papers were going fast, and the little colored boy's pockets were filling with the desired coins. It would have been all right with Jimmy if the policeman hadn't come up on him just as he was about to toss the "bones," and when Blinky Scott had him "faded" to the amount of five hard-earned pennies.

Well, they were trying to suppress youthful gambling in New York, and the officer had to do his duty. The others scuttled away, but Jimmy was so absorbed in the game that he didn't see the "cop" until he was right on him, so he was "pinched." He blubbered a little and wiped his grimy face with his grimier sleeve until it was one long, brown smear. You know this was Jimmy's first time.

The big blue-coat looked a little bit ashamed as he marched him down the street, followed at a distance by a few hooting boys. Some of the holiday shoppers turned to look at them as they passed and murmured, "Poor little chap; I wonder what he's been up to now." Others said sarcastically, "It seems strange that 'copper' didn't call for help." A few of his brother officers grinned at him as he passed, and he blushed, but the dignity of the law must be upheld and the crime of gambling among the newsboys was a growing evil.

Yes, the dignity of the law must be upheld, and though Jimmy was only a small boy, it would be well to make an example of him. So his name and age were put down on the blotter, and over against them the offence with which he was charged. Then he was locked up to await trial the next morning.

"It's shameful," the bearded sergeant said, "how the kids are carryin' on these days. People are feelin' pretty generous, an' they'll toss 'em a nickel er a dime fur their paper an' tell 'em to keep the change fur Christmas, an' foist thing you know the little beggars are shootin' craps er pitchin' pennies. We've got to make an example of some of 'em."

'Liza Ann Lewis was tearing through her work that day to get home and do her Christmas shopping, and she was singing as she worked some such old song as she used to sing in the good old days back home. She reached her room late and tired, but happy. Visions of a "wakening up" time for her and Jimmy were in her mind. But Jimmy wasn't there.

"I wunner whah that little scamp is," she said, smiling; "I tol' him to hu'y home, but I reckon he's stayin' out latah wid de evenin' papahs so's to bring home mo' money."

Hour after hour passed and he did not come; then she grew alarmed. At two o'clock in the morning she could stand it no longer and she went over and awakened Blinky Scott, much to that young gentleman's disgust, who couldn't see why any woman need make such a fuss about a kid. He told her laconically that "Chimmie was pinched fur t'rowin' de bones."

She heard with a sinking heart and went home to her own room to walk the floor all night and sob.

In the morning, with all her Christmas savings tied up in a handkerchief, she hurried down to Jefferson Market court room. There was a full blotter that morning, and the Judge was rushing through with it. He wanted to get home to his Christmas dinner. But he paused long enough when he got to Jimmy's case to deliver a brief but stern lecture upon the evil of child-gambling in New York. He said that as it was Christmas Day he would like to release the prisoner with a reprimand, but he thought that this had been done too often and that it was high time to make an example of one of the offenders.

Well, it was fine or imprisonment. 'Liza Ann struggled up through the crowd of spectators and her Christmas treasure added to what Jimmy had, paid his fine and they went out of the court room together.

When they were in their room again she put the boy to bed, for there was no fire and no coal to make one. Then she wrapped herself in a shabby shawl and sat huddled up over the empty stove.

Down in the alley she heard the voice of the day before singing:

"Oh, darkies, how my heart grows weary,
Far from the old folks at home."

And she burst into tears.

A MESS OF POTTAGE

It was because the Democratic candidate for Governor was such an energetic man that he had been able to stir Little Africa, which was a Republican stronghold, from centre to circumference. He was a man who believed in carrying the war into the enemy's country. Instead of giving them a chance to attack him, he went directly into their camp, leaving discontent and disaffection among their allies. He believed in his principles. He had faith in his policy for the government of the State, and, more than all, he had a convincing way of making others see as he saw.

No other Democrat had ever thought it necessary to assail the stronghold of Little Africa. He had merely put it into his forecast as "solidly against," sent a little money to be distributed desultorily in the district, and then left it to go its way, never doubting what that way would be. The opposing candidates never felt that the place was worthy of consideration, for as the Chairman of the Central Committee said, holding up his hand with the fingers close together: "What's the use of wasting any speakers down there? We've got 'em just like that."

It was all very different with Mr. Lane.

"Gentlemen," he said to the campaign managers, "that black district must not be ignored. Those people go one way because they are never invited to go another."

"Oh, I tell you now, Lane," said his closest friend, "it'll be a waste of material to send anybody down there. They simply go like a flock of sheep, and nothing is going to turn them."

"What's the matter with the bellwether?" said Lane sententiously.

"That's just exactly what *is* the matter. Their bellwether is an old deacon named Isham Swift, and you couldn't turn him with a forty-horsepower crank."

"There's nothing like trying."

"There are many things very similar to failing, but none so bad."

"I'm willing to take the risk."

"Well, all right; but whom will you send? We can't waste a good man."

"I'll go myself."

"What, you?"

"Yes, I."

"Why, you'd be the laughing-stock of the State."

"All right; put me down for that office if I never reach the gubernatorial chair."

"Say, Lane, what was the name of that Spanish fellow who went out to fight windmills, and all that sort of thing?"

"Never mind, Widner; you may be a good political hustler, but you're dead bad on your classics," said Lane laughingly.

So they put him down for a speech in Little Africa, because he himself desired it.

Widner had not lied to him about Deacon Swift, as he found when he tried to get the old man to preside at the meeting. The Deacon refused with indignation at the very idea. But others were more acquiescent, and Mount Moriah church was hired at a rental that made the Rev. Ebenezer Clay and all his Trustees rub their hands with glee and think well of the candidate. Also they looked at their shiny coats and thought of new suits.

There was much indignation expressed that Mount Moriah should have lent herself to such a cause, and there were murmurs even among the congregation where the Rev. Ebenezer Clay was usually an unquestioned autocrat. But, because Eve was the mother of all of us and the thing was so new, there was a great crowd on the night of the meeting. The Rev. Ebenezer Clay presided. Lane had said, "If I can't get the bellwether to jump the way I want, I'll transfer the bell." This he had tried to do. The effort was very like him.

The Rev. Mr. Clay, looking down into more frowning faces than he cared to see, spoke more boldly than he felt. He told his people that though they had their own opinions and ideas, it was well to hear both sides. He said, "The brothah," meaning the candidate, "had a few thoughts to pussent," and he hoped they'd listen to him quietly. Then he added subtly: "Of co'se Brothah Lane knows we colo'ed folks 're goin' to think our own way, anyhow."

The people laughed and applauded, and Lane went to his work. They were quiet and attentive. Every now and then some old brother grunted and shook his head. But in the main they merely listened.

Lane was pleasing, plausible and convincing, and the brass band which he had brought with him was especially effective. The audience left the church shaking their heads with a different meaning, and all the way home there were remarks such as, "He sholy tol' de truth," "Dat man was right," "They ain't no way to 'ny a word he said."

Just at that particular moment it looked very dark for the other candidate, especially as the brass band lingered around an hour or so and discoursed sweet music in the streets where the negroes most did congregate.

Twenty years ago such a thing could not have happened, but the ties which had bound the older generation irrevocably to one party were being loosed upon the younger men. The old men said "We know;" the young ones said "We have heard," and so there was hardly anything of the blind allegiance which had made even free thought seem treason to their fathers.

Now all of this was the reason of the great indignation that was rife in the breasts of other Little Africans and which culminated in a mass meeting called by Deacon Isham Swift and held at Bethel Chapel a few nights later. For two or three days before this congregation of the opposing elements there were ominous mutterings. On the streets little knots of negroes stood and told of the terrible thing that had taken place at Mount Moriah. Shoulders were grasped, heads were wagged and awful things prophesied as the result of this compromise with the general enemy. No one was louder in his denunciation of the treacherous course of the Rev. Ebenezer Clay than the Republican bellwether, Deacon Swift. He saw in it signs of the break-up of racial integrity and he bemoaned the tendency loud and long. His son Tom did not tell him that he had gone to the meeting himself and had been one of those to come out shaking his head in acquiescent doubt at the truths he had heard. But he went, as in duty bound, to his father's meeting.

The church was one thronging mass of colored citizens. On the platform, from which the pulpit had been removed, sat Deacon Swift and his followers. On each side of him were banners bearing glowing inscriptions. One of the banners which the schoolmistress had prepared read:

"His temples are our forts and towers which frown upon a tyrant foe."

The schoolmistress taught in a mixed school. They had mixed it by giving her a room in a white school where she had only colored pupils. Therefore she was loyal to her party, and was known as a woman of public spirit.

The meeting was an enthusiastic one, but no such demonstration was shown through it all as when old Deacon Swift himself arose to address the assembly. He put Moses Jackson in the chair, and then as he walked forward to the front of the platform a great, white-haired, rugged, black figure, he was heroic in his very crudeness. He wore a long, old Prince Albert coat, which swept carelessly about his thin legs. His turndown collar was disputing territory with his tie and his waistcoat. His head was down, and he glanced out of the lower part of his eyes over the congregation, while his hands fumbled at the sides of his trousers in an embarrassment which may have been pretended or otherwise.

"Mistah Cheerman," he said, "fu' myse'f, I ain't no speakah. I ain't nevah been riz up dat way. I has plowed an' I has sowed, an' latah on I has laid cyahpets, an' I has whitewashed. But, ladies an' gent'men, I is a man, an' as a man I want to speak to you ternight. We is lak a flock o' sheep, an' in de las' week de wolf has come among ouah midst. On evah side we has hyeahd de shephe'd dogs a-ba'kin' a-wa'nin' unto us. But, my f'en's, de cotton o' p'ospe'ity has been stuck in ouah eahs. Fu' thirty yeahs er mo', ef I do not disremember, we has walked de streets an' de by-ways o' dis country an' called ouahse'ves f'eemen. Away back yander, in de days of old, lak de chillen of Is'ul in Egypt, a deliv'ah came unto us, an Ab'aham Lincoln a-lifted de yoke f'om ouah shouldahs." The audience waked up and began swaying, and there was moaning heard from both Amen corners.

"But, my f'en's, I want to ax you, who was behind Ab'aham Lincoln? Who was it helt up dat man's han's when dey sent bayonets an' buttons to enfo'ce his word — umph? I want to — to know who was behin' him? Wasn' it de 'Publican pa'ty?" There were cries of "Yes, yes! dat's so!" One old sister rose and waved her sunbonnet.

"An' now I want to know in dis hyeah day o' comin' up ef we a-gwineter 'sert de ol' flag which waved ovah Lincoln, waved ovah Gin'r'l Butler, an' led us up straight to f'eedom? Ladies an' gent'men, an' my f'en's, I know dar have been suttain meetin's held lately in dis pa't o' de town. I know dar have been suttain cannerdates which have come down hyeah an' brung us de mixed wine o' Babylon. I know dar have been dem o' ouah own people who have drunk an' become drunk — ah! But I want to know, an' I want to ax you ternight as my f'en's an' my brothahs, is we all a-gwineter do it — huh? Is we all a-gwineter drink o' dat wine? Is we all a-gwineter reel down de perlitical street, a-staggerin' to an' fro? — hum!"

Cries of "No! No! No!" shook the whole church.

"Gent'men an' ladies," said the old man, lowering his voice, "de pa'able has been 'peated, an' some o' us — I ain't mentionin' no names, an' I ain't a-blamin' no chu'ch — but I say dar is some o' us dat has sol' dere buthrights fu' a pot o' cabbage."

What more Deacon Swift said is hardly worth the telling, for the whole church was in confusion and little more was heard. But he carried everything with him, and Lane's work seemed all undone. On a back seat of the church Tom Swift, the son of the presiding officer, sat and smiled at his father unmoved, because he had gone as far as the sixth grade in school, and thought he knew more.

As the reporters say, the meeting came to a close amid great enthusiasm.

The day of election came and Little Africa gathered as usual about the polls in the precinct. The Republicans followed their plan of not bothering about the district. They had heard of the Deacon's meeting, and chuckled to themselves in their committee-room. Little Africa was all solid, as usual, but

Lane was not done yet. His emissaries were about, as thick as insurance agents, and they, as well as the Republican workers, had money to spare and to spend. Some votes, which counted only for numbers, were fifty cents apiece, but when Tom Swift came down they knew who he was and what his influence could do. They gave him five dollars, and Lane had one more vote and a deal of prestige. The young man thought he was voting for his convictions.

He had just cast his ballot, and the crowd was murmuring around him still at the wonder of it — for the Australian ballot has tongues as well as ears — when his father came up, with two or three of his old friends, each with the old ticket in his hands. He heard the rumor and laughed. Then he came up to Tom.

"Huh," he said, "dey been sayin' 'roun' hyeah you voted de Democratic ticket. Go mek 'em out a lie."

"I did vote the Democratic ticket," said Tom steadily.

The old man fell back a step and gasped, as if he had been struck.

"You did?" he cried. "You did?"

"Yes," said Tom, visibly shaken; "every man has a right —"

"Evah man has a right to what?" cried the old man.

"To vote as he thinks he ought to," was his son's reply.

Deacon Swift's eyes were bulging and reddening.

"You — you tell me dat?" His slender form towered above his son's, and his knotted, toil-hardened hands opened and closed.

"You tell me dat? You with yo' bringin' up vote de way you think you're right? You lie! Tell me what dey paid you, or, befo' de Lawd, I'll taih you to pieces right hyeah!"

Tom wavered. He was weaker than his father. He had not gone through the same things, and was not made of the same stuff.

"They — they give me five dollahs," he said; "but it wa'n't fu' votin'."

"Fi' dollahs! fi' dollahs! My son sell hisse'f fu' fi' dollahs! an' forty yeahs ago I brung fifteen hun'erd, an' dat was only my body, but you sell body an' soul fu' fi' dollahs!"

Horror and scorn and grief and anger were in the old man's tone. Tears trickled down his wrinkled face, but there was no weakness in the grip with which he took hold of his son's arms.

"Tek it back to 'em!" he said. "Tek it back to 'em."

"But, pap —"

"Tek it back to 'em, I say, or yo' blood be on yo' own haid!"

And then, shamefaced before the crowd, driven by his father's anger, he went back to the man who had paid him and yielded up the precious bank-note. Then they turned, the one head-hung, the other proud in his very indignation, and made their way homeward.

There was prayer-meeting the next Wednesday night at Bethel Chapel. It was nearly over and the minister was about to announce the Doxology, when old Deacon Swift arose.

"Des' a minute, brothahs," he said. "I want to mek a 'fession. I was too ha'd an' too brash in my talk de othah night, an' de Lawd visited my sins upon my haid. He struck me in de bosom o' my own fambly. My own son went wrong. Pray fu' me!"

THE TRUSTFULNESS OF POLLY

Polly Jackson was a model woman. She was practical and hard-working. She knew the value of a dollar, could make one and keep one, sometimes — fate permitting. Fate was usually Sam and Sam was Polly's husband. Any morning at six o'clock she might be seen, basket on arm, wending her way to the homes of her wealthy patrons for the purpose of bringing in their washing, for by this means did she gain her livelihood. She had been a person of hard common sense, which suffered its greatest lapse when she allied herself with the man whose name she bore. After that the lapses were more frequent.

How she could ever have done so no one on earth could tell. Sam was her exact opposite. He was an easy-going, happy-go-lucky individual, who worked only when occasion demanded and inclination and the weather permitted. The weather was usually more acquiescent than inclination. He was sanguine of temperament, highly imaginative and a dreamer of dreams. Indeed, he just missed being a poet. A man who dreams takes either to poetry or policy. Not being able quite to reach the former, Sam had declined upon the latter, and, instead of meter, feet and rhyme, his mind was taken up with "hosses," "gigs" and "straddles."

He was always "jes' behin' dem policy sha'ks, an' I'll be boun', Polly, but I gwine to ketch 'em dis time."

Polly heard this and saw the same result so often that even her stalwart faith began to turn into doubt. But Sam continued to reassure her and promise that some day luck would change. "An' when hit do change," he would add, impressively, "it's gwine change fu' sho', an' we'll have one wakenin' up time. Den I bet you'll git dat silk dress you been wantin' so long."

Polly did have ambitions in the direction of some such finery, and this plea always melted her. Trust was restored again, and Hope resumed her accustomed place.

It was, however, not through the successful culmination of any of Sam's policy manipulations that the opportunity at last came to Polly to realize her ambitions. A lady for whom she worked had a second-hand silk dress, which she was willing to sell cheap. Another woman had spoken for it, but if Polly could get the money in three weeks she would let her have it for seven dollars.

To say that the companion of Sam Jackson jumped at the offer hardly indicates the attitude of eagerness with which she received the proposition.

"Yas'm, I kin sholy git dat much money together in th'ee weeks de way I's a-wo'kin'."

"Well, now, Polly, be sure; for if you are not prompt I shall have to dispose of it where it was first promised," was the admonition.

"Oh, you kin 'pend on me, Mis' Mo'ton; fu' when I sets out to save money I kin save, I tell you." Polly was not usually so sanguine, but what changes will not the notion of the possession of a brown silk dress trimmed with passementrie make in the disposition of a woman?

Polly let Sam into the secret, and, be it said to his credit, he entered into the plan with an enthusiasm no less intense than her own. He had always wanted to see her in a silk dress, he told her, and then in a quizzically injured tone of voice, "but you ought to waited tell I ketched dem policy sha'ks an' I'd 'a' got you a new one." He even went so far as to go to work for a week and bring Polly his earnings, of course, after certain "little debts" which he mentioned but did not specify, had been deducted.

But in spite of all this, when washing isn't bringing an especially good price; when one must eat and food is high; when a grasping landlord comes around once every week and exacts tribute for the privilege of breathing foul air from an alley in a room up four flights; when, I say, all this is true, and it generally is true in the New York tenderloin, seven whole dollars are not easily saved. There was much raking and scraping and pinching during each day that at night Polly might add a few nickels or pennies to the store that jingled in a blue jug in one corner of her closet. She called it her bank, and Sam had laughed at the conceit, telling her that that was one bank anyhow that couldn't "bust."

As the days went on how she counted her savings and exulted in their growth! She already saw herself decked out in her new gown, the envy and admiration of every woman in the neighborhood. She even began to wish that she had a full-length glass in order that she might get the complete effect of her own magnificence. So saving, hoping, dreaming, the time went on until a few days before the limit, and there was only about a dollar to be added to make the required amount. This she could do easily in the remaining time. So Polly was jubilant.

Now everything would have been all right and matters would have ended happily if Sam had only kept on at work. But, no. He must needs stop, and give his mind the chance to be employed with other things. And that is just what happened. For about this time, having nothing else to do, like that old king of Bible renown, he dreamed a dream. But unlike the royal dreamer, he asked no seer or prophet to interpret his dream to him. He merely drove his hand down into his inside pocket, and fished up an ancient dream-book, greasy and tattered with use. Over this he pored until his eyes bulged and his hands shook with excitement.

"Got 'em at last!" he exclaimed. "Dey ain't no way fu' dem to git away f'om me. I's behind 'em. I's behind 'em I tell you," and then his face fell and he sat for a long time with his chin in his hand thinking, thinking.

"Polly," said he when his wife came in, "d'you know what I dremp 'bout las' night?"

"La! Sam Jackson, you ain't gone to dreamin' agin. I thought you done quit all dat foolishness."

"Now jes' listen at you runnin' on. You ain't never axed me what I dremp 'bout yit."

"Hit don' make much diffunce to me, less 'n you kin dream 'bout a dollah mo' into my pocket."

"Dey has been sich things did," said Sam sententiously. He got up and went out. If there is one thing above another that your professional dreamer does demand, it is appreciation. Sam had failed to get it from Polly, but he found a balm for all his hurts when he met Bob Davis.

"What!" exclaimed Bob. "Dreamed of a nakid black man. Fu' de Lawd sake, Sam, don' let de chance pass. You got 'em dis time sho'. I'll put somep'n' on it myse'f. Wha'd you think ef we'd win de 'capital'?"

That was enough. The two parted and Sam hurried home. He crept into the house. Polly was busy hanging clothes on the roof. Where now are the guardian spirits that look after the welfare of trusting women? Where now are the enchanted belongings that even in the hands of the thief cry out to their unsuspecting owners? Gone. All gone with the ages of faith that gave them birth. Without an outcry, without even so much as a warning jingle, the contents of the blue jug and the embodied hope of a woman's heart were transferred to the gaping pocket of Sam Jackson. Polly went on hanging up clothes on the roof.

Sam chuckled to himself: "She won't never have a chanst to scol' me. I'll git de drawin's early dis evenin', an' go ma'chin' home wif a new silk fu' huh, an' money besides. I do' want my wife waihin' no white folks' secon'-han' clothes nohow. My, but won't she be su'prised an' tickled. I kin jes' see huh now. Oh, mistah policy-sha'k, I got you now. I been layin' fu' you fu' a long time, but you's my meat at las'."

He marched into the policy shop like a conqueror. To the amazement of the clerk, he turned out a pocketful of small coin on the table and played it all in "gigs," "straddles and combinations."

"I'll call on you about ha' pas' fou', Mr. McFadden," he announced exultantly as he went out.

"Faith, sor," said McFadden to his colleague, "if that nagur does ketch it he'll break us, sure."

Sam could hardly wait for half-past four. A minute before the time he burst in upon McFadden and demanded the drawings. They were handed to him. He held his breath as his eye went down the column of figures. Then he gasped and staggered weakly out of the room. The policy sharks had triumphed again.

Sam walked the streets until nine o'clock that night. He was afraid to go home to Polly. He knew that she had been to the jug and found — . He groaned, but at last his very helplessness drove him in. Polly, with swollen eyes, was sitting by the table, the empty jug lying on its side before her.

"Sam," she exclaimed, "whaih's my money? Whaih's my money I been wo'kin' fu' all dis time?"

"Why — Why, Polly —"

"Don' go beatin' 'roun' de bush. I want 'o know whaih my money is; you tuck it."

"Polly, I dremp —"

"I do' keer what you dremp, I want my money fu' my dress."

His face was miserable.

"I thought sho' dem numbers 'u'd come out, an' —"

The woman flung herself upon the floor and burst into a storm of tears. Sam bent over her. "Nemmine, Polly," he said. "Nemmine. I thought I'd su'prise you. Dey beat me dis time." His teeth clenched. "But when I ketch dem policy sha'ks —"

THE TRAGEDY AT THREE FORKS

It was a drizzly, disagreeable April night. The wind was howling in a particularly dismal and malignant way along the valleys and hollows of that part of Central Kentucky in which the rural settlement of Three Forks is situated. It had been "trying to rain" all day in a half-hearted sort of manner, and now the drops were flying about in a cold spray. The night was one of dense, inky blackness, occasionally relieved by flashes of lightning. It was hardly a night on which a girl should be out. And yet one was out, scudding before the storm, with clenched teeth and wild eyes, wrapped head and shoulders in a great blanket shawl, and looking, as she sped along like a restless, dark ghost. For her, the night and the storm had no terrors; passion had driven out fear. There was determination in her every movement, and purpose was apparent in the concentration of energy with which she set her foot down. She drew the shawl closer about her head with a convulsive grip, and muttered with a half sob, "'Tain't the first time, 'tain't the first time she's tried to take me down in comp'ny, but —" and the sob gave way to the dry, sharp note in her voice, "I'll fix her, if it kills me. She thinks I ain't her ekals, does she? 'Cause her pap's got money, an' has good crops on his lan', an' my pap ain't never had no luck, but I'll show 'er, I'll show 'er that good luck can't allus last. Pleg-take 'er, she's jealous, 'cause I'm better lookin' than she is, an' pearter in every way, so she tries to make me little in the eyes of people. Well, you'll find out what it is to be pore — to have nothin', Seliny Williams, if you live."

The black night hid a gleam in the girl's eyes, and her shawl hid a bundle of something light, which she clutched very tightly, and which smelled of kerosene.

The dark outline of a house and its outbuildings loomed into view through the dense gloom; and the increased caution with which the girl proceeded, together with the sudden breathless intentness of her conduct, indicated that it was with this house and its occupants she was concerned.

The house was cellarless, but it was raised at the four corners on heavy blocks, leaving a space between the ground and the floor, the sides of which were partly closed by banks of ashes and earth which were thrown up against the weather-boarding. It was but a few minutes' work to scrape away a portion of this earth, and push under the pack of shavings into which the mysterious bundle resolved itself. A match was lighted, sheltered, until it blazed, and then dropped among them. It took only a short walk and a shorter time to drop a handful of burning shavings into the hay at the barn. Then the girl turned and sped away, muttering: "I reckon I've fixed you, Seliny Williams, mebbe, next time you meet me out at a dance, you won't snub me; mebbe next time, you'll be ez pore ez I am, an'll be willin' to dance crost from even ole 'Lias Hunster's gal."

The constantly falling drizzle might have dampened the shavings and put out the fire, had not the wind fanned the sparks into too rapid a flame, which caught eagerly at shingle, board and joist until house and barn were wrapped in flames. The whinnying of the horses first woke Isaac Williams, and he sprang from bed at sight of the furious light which surrounded his house. He got his family up and out of the house, each seizing what he could of wearing apparel as he fled before the flames. Nothing else could be saved, for the fire had gained terrible headway, and its fierceness precluded all possibility of fighting it. The neighbors attracted by the lurid glare came from far and near, but the fire had done its work, and their efforts availed nothing. House, barn, stock, all, were a mass of ashes and charred cinders. Isaac Williams, who had a day before, been accounted one of the solidest farmers in the region, went out that night with his family — homeless.

Kindly neighbors took them in, and by morning the news had spread throughout all the country-side. Incendiarism was the only cause that could be assigned, and many were the speculations as to who the guilty party could be. Of course, Isaac Williams had enemies. But who among them was mean, ay, daring enough to perpetrate such a deed as this?

Conjecture was rife, but futile, until old 'Lias Hunster, who though he hated Williams, was shocked at the deed, voiced the popular sentiment by saying, "Look a here, folks, I tell you that's the work o' niggers, I kin see their hand in it."

"Niggers, o' course," exclaimed every one else. "Why didn't we think of it before? It's jest like 'em."

Public opinion ran high and fermented until Saturday afternoon when the county paper brought the whole matter to a climax by coming out in a sulphurous account of the affair, under the scarehead:

A TERRIBLE OUTRAGE!

MOST DASTARDLY DEED EVER COMMITTED IN THE HISTORY OF
BARLOW COUNTY. A HIGHLY RESPECTED, UNOFFENDING
AND WELL-BELOVED FAMILY BURNED OUT OF HOUSE
AND HOME. NEGROES! UNDOUBTEDLY THE
PERPETRATORS OF THE DEED!

The article went on to give the facts of the case, and many more supposed facts, which had originated entirely in the mind of the correspondent. Among these facts was the intelligence that some strange negroes had been seen lurking in the vicinity the day before the catastrophe and that a party of citizens and farmers were scouring the surrounding country in search of them. "They would, if caught," concluded the correspondent, "be summarily dealt with."

Notwithstanding the utter falsity of these statements, it did not take long for the latter part of the article to become a prophecy fulfilled, and soon, excited, inflamed and misguided parties of men and boys were scouring the woods and roads in search of strange "niggers." Nor was it long, before one of the parties raised the cry that they had found the culprits. They had come upon two strange negroes going through the woods, who seeing a band of mounted and armed men, had instantly taken to their heels. This one act had accused, tried and convicted them.

The different divisions of the searching party came together, and led the negroes with ropes around their necks into the centre of the village. Excited crowds on the one or two streets which the hamlet boasted, cried "Lynch 'em, lynch 'em! Hang the niggers up to the first tree!"

Jane Hunster was in one of the groups, as the shivering negroes passed, and she turned very pale even under the sunburn that browned her face.

The law-abiding citizens of Barlow County, who composed the capturing party, were deaf to the admonitions of the crowd. They filed solemnly up the street, and delivered their prisoners to the keeper of the jail, sheriff, by courtesy, and scamp by the seal of Satan; and then quietly dispersed. There was something ominous in their very orderliness.

Late that afternoon, the man who did duty as prosecuting attorney for that county, visited the prisoners at the jail, and drew from them the story that they were farm-laborers from an adjoining county. They had come over only the day before, and were passing through on the quest for work; the bad weather and the lateness of the season having thrown them out at home.

"Uh, huh," said the prosecuting attorney at the conclusion of the tale, "your story's all right, but the only trouble is that it won't do here. They won't believe you. Now, I'm a friend to niggers as much as any white man can be, if they'll only be friends to themselves, an' I want to help you two all I can. There's only one way out of this trouble. You must confess that you did this."

"But Mistah," said the bolder of the two negroes, "how kin we 'fess, when we wasn' nowhahs nigh de place?"

"Now there you go with regular nigger stubbornness; didn't I tell you that that was the only way out of this? If you persist in saying you didn't do it, they'll hang you; whereas, if you own, you'll only get a couple of years in the 'pen.' Which 'ud you rather have, a couple o' years to work out, or your necks stretched?"

"Oh, we'll 'fess, Mistah, we'll 'fess we done it; please, please don't let 'em hang us!" cried the thoroughly frightened blacks.

"Well, that's something like it," said the prosecuting attorney as he rose to go. "I'll see what can be done for you."

With marvelous and mysterious rapidity, considering the reticence which a prosecuting attorney who was friendly to the negroes should display, the report got abroad that the negroes had confessed their crime, and soon after dark, ominous looking crowds began to gather in the streets. They passed and repassed the place, where stationed on the little wooden shelf that did duty as a doorstep, Jane Hunster sat with her head buried in her hands. She did not raise up to look at any of them, until a hand was laid on her shoulder, and a voice called her, "Jane!"

"Oh, hit's you, is it, Bud," she said, raising her head slowly, "howdy?"

"Howdy yoreself," said the young man, looking down at her tenderly.

"Bresh off yore pants an' set down," said the girl making room for him on the step. The young man did so, at the same time taking hold of her hand with awkward tenderness.

"Jane," he said, "I jest can't wait fur my answer no longer! you got to tell me tonight, either one way or the other. Dock Heaters has been a-blowin' hit aroun' that he has beat my time with you. I don't believe it Jane, fur after keepin' me waitin' all these years, I don't believe you'd go back on me. You know I've allus loved you, ever sence we was little children together."

The girl was silent until he leaned over and said in pleading tones, "What do you say, Jane?"

"I hain't fitten fur you, Bud."

"Don't talk that-a-way, Jane, you know ef you jest say 'yes,' I'll be the happiest man in the state."

"Well, yes, then, Bud, for you're my choice, even ef I have fooled with you fur a long time; an' I'm glad now that I kin make somebody happy." The girl was shivering, and her hands were cold, but she made no movement to rise or enter the house.

Bud put his arms around her and kissed her shyly. And just then a shout arose from the crowd down the street.

"What's that?" she asked.

"It's the boys gittin' worked up, I reckon. They're going to lynch them niggers tonight that burned ole man Williams out."

The girl leaped to her feet, "They mustn't do it," she cried. "They ain't never been tried!"

"Set down, Janey," said her lover, "they've owned up to it."

"I don't believe it," she exclaimed, "somebody's jest a lyin' on 'em to git 'em hung because they're niggers."

"Sh — Jane, you're excited, you ain't well; I noticed that when I first come tonight. Somebody's got to suffer fur that house-burnin', an' it might ez well be them ez anybody else. You mustn't talk so. Ef people knowed you wuz a standin' up fur niggers so, it 'ud ruin you."

He had hardly finished speaking, when the gate opened, and another man joined them.

"Hello, there, Dock Heaters, that you?" said Bud Mason.

"Yes, it's me. How are you, Jane?" said the newcomer.

"Oh, jest middlin', Dock, I ain't right well."

"Well, you might be in better business than settin' out here talkin' to Bud Mason."

"Don't know how as to that," said his rival, "seein' as we're engaged."

"You're a liar!" flashed Dock Heaters.

Bud Mason half rose, then sat down again; his triumph was sufficient without a fight. To him "liar" was a hard name to swallow without resort to blows, but he only said, his flashing eyes belying his calm tone, "Mebbe I am a liar, jest ast Jane."

"Is that the truth, Jane?" asked Heaters, angrily.

"Yes, hit is, Dock Heaters, an' I don't see what you've got to say about it; I hain't never promised you nothin' shore."

Heaters turned toward the gate without a word. Bud sent after him a mocking laugh, and the bantering words, "You'd better go down, an' he'p hang them niggers, that's all you're good fur." And the rival really did bend his steps in that direction.

Another shout arose from the throng down the street, and rising hastily, Bud Mason exclaimed, "I must be goin', that yell means business."

"Don't go down there, Bud!" cried Jane. "Don't go, fur my sake, don't go." She stretched out her arms, and clasped them about his neck.

"You don't want me to miss nothin' like that," he said as he unclasped her arms; "don't you be worried, I'll be back past here." And in a moment he was gone, leaving her cry of "Bud, Bud, come back," to smite the empty silence.

When Bud Mason reached the scene of action, the mob had already broken into the jail and taken out the trembling prisoners. The ropes were round their necks and they had been led to a tree.

"See ef they'll do anymore house-burnin'!" cried one as the ends of the ropes were thrown over the limbs of the tree.

"Reckon they'll like dancin' hemp a heap better," mocked a second.

"Justice an' pertection!" yelled a third.

"The mills of the gods grind swift enough in Barlow County," said the schoolmaster.

The scene, the crowd, the flaring lights and harsh voices intoxicated Mason, and he was soon the most enthusiastic man in the mob. At the word, his was one of the willing hands that seized the rope, and jerked the negroes off their feet into eternity. He joined the others with savage glee as they emptied their revolvers into the bodies. Then came the struggle for pieces of the rope as "keepsakes." The scramble was awful. Bud Mason had just laid hold of a piece and cut it off, when some one laid hold of the other end. It was not at the rope's end, and the other man also used his knife in getting a hold. Mason looked up to see who his antagonist was, and his face grew white with anger. It was Dock Heaters.

"Let go this rope," he cried.

"Let go yoreself, I cut it first, an' I'm a goin' to have it."

They tugged and wrestled and panted, but they were evenly matched and neither gained the advantage.

"Let go, I say," screamed Heaters, wild with rage.

"I'll die first, you dirty dog!"

The words were hardly out of his mouth before a knife flashed in the light of the lanterns, and with a sharp cry, Bud Mason fell to the ground. Heaters turned to fly, but strong hands seized and disarmed him.

"He's killed him! Murder, murder!" arose the cry, as the crowd with terror-stricken faces gathered about the murderer and his victim.

"Lynch him!" suggested some one whose thirst for blood was not yet appeased.

"No," cried an imperious voice, "who knows what may have put him up to it? Give a white man a chance for his life."

The crowd parted to let in the town marshal and the sheriff who took charge of the prisoner, and led him to the little rickety jail, whence he escaped later that night; while others improvised a litter, and bore the dead man to his home.

The news had preceded them up the street, and reached Jane's ears. As they passed her home, she gazed at them with a stony, vacant stare, muttering all the while as she rocked herself to and fro, "I knowed it, I knowed it!"

The press was full of the double lynching and the murder. Conservative editors wrote leaders about it in which they deplored the rashness of the hanging but warned the negroes that the only way to stop lynching was to quit the crimes of which they so often stood accused. But only in one little obscure sheet did an editor think to say, "There was Salem and its witchcraft; there is the south and its lynching. When the blind frenzy of a people condemn a man as soon as he is accused, his enemies need not look far for a pretext!"

THE FINDING OF ZACH

The rooms of the "Banner" Club — an organization of social intent, but with political streaks — were a blaze of light that Christmas Eve night. On the lower floor some one was strumming on the piano, and upstairs, where the "ladies" sat, and where the Sunday smokers were held, a man was singing one of the latest coon songs. The "Banner" always got them first, mainly because the composers went there, and often the air of the piece itself had been picked out or patched together, with the help of the "Banner's" piano, before the song was taken out for somebody to set the "'companiment" to it.

The proprietor himself had just gone into the parlor to see that the Christmas decorations were all that he intended them to be when a door opened and an old man entered the room. In one hand he carried an ancient carpetbag, which he deposited on the floor, while he stared around at the grandeur of the place. He was a typical old uncle of the South, from the soles of his heavy brogans to the shiny top of his bald pate, with its fringe of white wool. It was plain to be seen that he was not a denizen of the town, or of that particular quarter. They do not grow old in the Tenderloin. He paused long enough to take in the appointments of the place, then, suddenly remembering his manners, he doffed his hat and bowed with old-fashioned courtesy to the splendid proprietor.

"Why, how'do, uncle!" said the genial Mr. Turner, extending his hand. "Where did you stray from?"

"Howdy, son, howdy," returned the old man gravely. "I hails f'om Miss'ippi myse'f, a mighty long ways f'om hyeah."

His voice and old-time intonation were good to listen to, and Mr. Turner's thoughts went back to an earlier day in his own life. He was from Maryland himself. He drew up a chair for the old man and took one himself. A few other men passed into the room and stopped to look with respectful amusement at the visitor. He was such a perfect bit of old plantation life and so obviously out of place in a Tenderloin club room.

"Well, uncle, are you looking for a place to stay?" pursued Turner.

"Not 'zackly, honey; not 'zackly. I come up hyeah a-lookin' fu' a son o' mine dat been away f'om home nigh on to five years. He live hyeah in Noo Yo'k, an' dey tell me whaih I 'quiahed dat I li'ble to fin' somebody hyeah dat know him. So I jes' drapped in."

"I know a good many young men from the South. What's your son's name?"

"Well, he named aftah my ol' mastah, Zachariah Priestley Shackelford."

"Zach Shackelford!" exclaimed some of the men, and there was a general movement among them, but a glance from Turner quieted the commotion.

"Why, yes, I know your son," he said. "He's in here almost every night, and he's pretty sure to drop in a little later on. He has been singing with one of the colored companies here until a couple of weeks ago."

"Heish up; you don't say so. Well! well! well! but den Zachariah allus did have a mighty sweet voice. He tu'k hit aftah his mammy. Well, I sholy is hopin' to see dat boy. He was allus my favorite, aldough I reckon a body ain' got no livin' right to have favorites among dey chilluns. But Zach was allus sich a good boy."

The men turned away. They could not remember a time since they had known Zach Shackelford when by any stretch of imagination he could possibly have been considered good. He was known as one of the wildest young bucks that frequented the club, with a deft hand at cards and dice and a smooth throat for whisky. But Turner gave them such a defiant glance that they were almost ready to subscribe to anything the old man might say.

"Dis is a mighty fine place you got hyeah. Hit mus' be a kind of a hotel or boa'din' house, ain't hit?"

"Yes, something like."

"We don' have nuffin' lak dis down ouah way. Co'se, we's jes' common folks. We wo'ks out in de fiel', and dat's about all we knows — fiel', chu'ch an' cabin. But I's mighty glad my Zach 's gittin' up in de worl'. He nevah were no great han' fu' wo'k. Hit kin' o' seemed to go agin his natur'. You know dey is folks lak dat."

"Lots of 'em, lots of 'em," said Mr. Turner.

The crowd of men had been augmented by a party from out of the card room, and they were listening intently to the old fellow's chatter. They felt now that they ought to laugh, but somehow they could not, and the twitching of their careless faces was not from suppressed merriment.

The visitor looked around at them, and then remarked: "My, what a lot of boa'dahs you got."

"They don't all stay here," answered Turner seriously; "some of them have just dropped in to see their friends."

"Den I 'low Zach'll be drappin' in presently. You mus' 'scuse me fu' talkin' 'bout him, but I's mighty anxious to clap my eyes on him. I's been gittin' on right sma't dese las' two yeahs, an' my ol' ooman she daid an' gone, an' I kin' o' lonesome, so I jes' p'omised mysef dis Crismus de gif' of a sight o' Zach. Hit do look foolish fu' a man ez ol' ez me to be a runnin' 'roun' de worl' a spen'in' money dis away, but hit do seem so ha'd to git Zach home."

"How long are you going to be with us?"

"Well, I 'specs to stay all o' Crismus week."

"Maybe —" began one of the men. But Turner interrupted him. "This gentleman is my guest. Uncle," turning to the old man, "do you ever — would you — er. I've got some pretty good liquor here, ah —"

Zach's father smiled a sly smile. "I do' know, suh," he said, crossing his leg high. "I's Baptis' mys'f, but 'long o' dese Crismus holidays I's right fond of a little toddy."

A half dozen eager men made a break for the bar, but Turner's uplifted hand held them. He was an autocrat in his way.

"Excuse me, gentlemen," he said, "but I think I remarked some time ago that Mr. Shackelford was my guest." And he called the waiter.

All the men had something and tapped rims with the visitor.

"'Pears to me you people is mighty clevah up hyeah; 'tain' no wondah Zachariah don' wan' to come home."

Just then they heard a loud whoop outside the door, and a voice broke in upon them singing thickly, "Oh, this spo'tin' life is surely killin' me." The men exchanged startled glances. Turner looked at them, and there was a command in his eye. Several of them hurried out, and he himself arose, saying: "I've got to go out for a little while, but you just make yourself at home, uncle. You can lie down right there on that sofa and push that button there — see, this way — if you want some more toddy. It shan't cost you anything."

"Oh, I'll res' myself, but I ain' gwine sponge on you dat away. I got some money," and the old man dug down into his long pocket. But his host laid a hand on his arm.

"Your money's no good up here."

"Wh — wh — why, I thought dis money passed any whah in de Nunited States!" exclaimed the bewildered old man.

"That's all right, but you can't spend it until we run out."

"Oh! Why, bless yo' soul, suh, you skeered me. You sho' is clevah."

Turner went out and came upon his emissaries, where they had halted the singing Zach in the hallway, and were trying to get into his muddled brain that his father was there.

"Wha'sh de ol' man doin' at de 'Banner,' gittin' gay in his ol' days? Hic."

That was enough for Turner to hear. "Look a-here," he said, "don't you get flip when you meet your father. He's come a long ways to see you, and I'm damned if he shan't see you right. Remember you're stoppin' at my house as long as the old man stays, and if you make a break while he's here I'll spoil your mug for you. Bring him along, boys."

Zach had started in for a Christmas celebration, but they took him into an empty room. They sent to the drug store and bought many things. When the young man came out an hour later he was straight, but sad.

"Why, Pap," he said when he saw the old man, "I'll be —"

"Hem!" said Turner.

"I'll be blessed!" Zach finished.

The old man looked him over. "Tsch! tsch! tsch! Dis is a Crismus gif' fu' sho'!" His voice was shaking. "I's so glad to see you, honey; but chile, you smell lak a 'pothac'ay shop."

"I ain't been right well lately," said Zach sheepishly.

To cover his confusion Turner called for eggnog.

When it came the old man said: "Well, I's Baptis' myse'f, but seein' it's Crismus —"

JOHNSONHAM, JUNIOR

Now any one will agree with me that it is entirely absurd for two men to fall out about their names; but then, circumstances alter cases. It had its beginning in 1863, and it has just ended.

In the first place, Ike and Jim had been good friends on the plantation, but when the time came for them to leave and seek homes for themselves each wanted a name. The master's name was Johnson, and they both felt themselves entitled to it. When Ike went forth to men as Isaac Johnson, and Jim, not to be outdone, became James Johnsonham, the rivalry began. Each married and became the father of a boy who took his father's name.

When both families moved North and settled in Little Africa their children had been taught that there must be eternal enmity between them on account of their names, and just as lasting a friendship on every other score. But with boys it was natural that the rivalry should extend to other things. When they went to school it was a contest for leadership both in the classroom and in sports, and when Isaac Johnson left school to go to work in the brickyard, James Johnsonham, not to be outdone in industry, also entered the same field of labor.

Later, it was questioned all up and down Douglass Street, which, by the way, is the social centre of Little Africa — as to which of the two was the better dancer or the more gallant beau. It was a piece of good fortune that they did not fall in love with the same girl and bring their rivalry into their affairs of the heart, for they were only men, and nothing could have kept them friends. But they came quite as near it as they could, for Matilda Benson was as bright a girl as Martha Mason, and when Ike married her she was an even-running contestant with her friend, Martha, for the highest social honors of their own particular set.

It was a foregone conclusion that when they were married and settled they should live near each other. So the houses were distant from each other only two or three doors. It was because every one knew every one else's business in that locality that Sandy Worthington took it upon himself to taunt the two men about their bone of contention.

"Mr. Johnson," he would say, when, coming from the down-town store where he worked, he would meet the two coming from their own labors in the brickyard, "how are you an' Mistah Johnsonham mekin' it ovah yo' names?"

"Well, I don' know that Johnsonham is so much of a name," Ike would say; and Jim would reply: "I 'low it's mo' name than Johnson, anyhow."

"So is stealin' ham mo' than stealin'," was the other's rejoinder, and then his friends would double up with mirth.

Sometimes the victorious repartee was Jim's, and then the laugh was on the other side. But the two went at it all good-naturedly, until one day, one foolish day, when they had both stopped too often on the way home, Jim grew angry at some little fling of his friend's, and burst into hot abuse of him. At first Ike was only astonished, and then his eyes, red with the dust of the brick-field, grew redder, the veins of his swarthy face swelled, and with a "Take that, Mistah Johnsonham," he gave Jim a resounding thwack across the face.

It took only a little time for a crowd to gather, and, with their usual tormentor to urge them on, the men forgot themselves and went into the fight in dead earnest. It was a hard-fought battle. Both rolled in the dust, caught at each other's short hair, pummeled, bit and swore. They were still rolling and tumbling when their wives, apprised of the goings on, appeared upon the scene and marched them home.

After that, because they were men, they kept a sullen silence between them, but Matilda and Martha, because they were women, had much to say to each other, and many unpleasant epithets to hurl and hurl again across the two yards that intervened between them. Finally, neither little family spoke to the other. And then, one day, there was a great bustle about Jim's house. A wise old woman went waddling in, and later the doctor came. That night the proud husband and father was treating his friends, and telling them it was a boy, and his name was to be James Johnsonham, Junior.

For a week Jim was irregular and unsteady in his habits, when one night, full of gin and pride, he staggered up to a crowd which was surrounding his rival, and said in a loud voice, "James Johnsonham, Junior — how does that strike you?"

"Any bettah than Isaac Johnson, Junior?" asked some one, slapping the happy Ike on the shoulder as the crowd burst into a loud guffaw. Jim's head was sadly bemuddled, and for a time he gazed upon the faces about him in bewilderment. Then a light broke in upon his mind, and with a "Whoo-ee!" he said, "No!" Ike grinned a defiant grin at him, and led the way to the nearest place where he and his friends might celebrate.

Jim went home to his wife full of a sullen, heavy anger. "Ike Johnson got a boy at his house, too," he said, "an' he done put Junior to his name." Martha raised her head from the pillow and hugged her own baby to her breast closer.

"It do beat all," she made answer airily; "we can't do a blessed thing but them thaih Johnsons has to follow right in ouah steps. Anyhow, I don't believe their baby is no sich healthy lookin' chile as this one is, bress his little hea't! 'Cause I knows Matilda Benson nevah was any too strong."

She was right; Matilda Benson was not so strong. The doctor went oftener to Ike's house than he had gone to Jim's, and three or four days after an undertaker went in.

They tried to keep the news from Martha's ears, but somehow it leaked into them, and when Jim came home on that evening she looked into her husband's face with a strange, new expression.

"Oh, Jim," she cried weakly, "'Tildy done gone, an' me jes' speakin' ha'd 'bout huh a little while ago, an' that po' baby lef thaih to die! Ain't it awful?"

"Nev' min'," said Jim, huskily; "nev' min', honey." He had seen Ike's face when the messenger had come for him at the brickyard, and the memory of it was like a knife at his heart.

"Jes' think, I said, only a day or so ago," Martha went on, "that 'Tildy wasn't strong; an' I was glad of it, Jim, I was glad of it! I was jealous of huh havin' a baby, too. Now she's daid, an' I feel jes' lak I'd killed huh. S'p'osin' God 'ud sen' a jedgment on me — s'p'osin' He'd take our little Jim?"

"Sh, sh, honey," said Jim, with a man's inadequacy in such a moment. "'Tain't yo' fault; you nevah wished huh any ha'm."

"No; but I said it, I said it!"

"Po' Ike," said Jim absently; "po' fellah!"

"Won't you go thaih," she asked, "an' see what you kin do fu' him?"

"He don't speak to me."

"You mus' speak to him; you got to do it, Jim; you got to."

"What kin I say? 'Tildy's daid."

She reached up and put her arms around her husband's brawny neck. "Go bring that po' little lamb hyeah," she said. "I kin save it, an' 'ten' to two. It'll be a sort of consolation fu' him to keep his chile."

"Kin you do that, Marthy?" he said. "Kin you do that?"

"I know I kin." A great load seemed to lift itself from Jim's heart as he burst out of the house. He opened Ike's door without knocking. The man sat by the empty fireplace with his head bowed over the ashes.

"Ike," he said, and then stopped.

Ike raised his head and glanced at him with a look of dull despair. "She's gone," he replied; "'Tildy's gone." There was no touch of anger in his tone. It was as if he took the visit for granted. All petty emotions had passed away before this great feeling which touched both earth and the beyond.

"I come fu' the baby," said Jim. "Marthy, she'll take keer of it."

He reached down and found the other's hand, and the two hard palms closed together in a strong grip. "Ike," he went on, "I'm goin' to drop the 'Junior' an' the 'ham,' an' the two little ones'll jes' grow up togethah, one o' them lak the othah."

The bereaved husband made no response. He only gripped the hand tighter. A little while later Jim came hastily from the house with something small wrapped closely in a shawl.

THE FAITH CURE MAN

Hope is tenacious. It goes on living and working when science has dealt it what should be its deathblow.

In the close room at the top of the old tenement house little Lucy lay wasting away with a relentless disease. The doctor had said at the beginning of the winter that she could not live. Now he said that he could do no more for her except to ease the few days that remained for the child.

But Martha Benson would not believe him. She was confident that doctors were not infallible. Anyhow, this one wasn't, for she saw life and health ahead for her little one.

Did not the preacher at the Mission Home say: "Ask, and ye shall receive?" and had she not asked and asked again the life of her child, her last and only one, at the hands of Him whom she worshipped?

No, Lucy was not going to die. What she needed was country air and a place to run about in. She had been housed up too much; these long Northern winters were too severe for her, and that was what made her so pinched and thin and weak. She must have air, and she should have it.

"Po' little lammie," she said to the child, "Mammy's little gal boun' to git well. Mammy gwine sen' huh out in de country when the spring comes, whaih she kin roll in de grass an' pick flowers an' git good an' strong. Don' baby want to go to de country? Don' baby want to see de sun shine?" And the child had looked up at her with wide, bright eyes, tossed her thin arms and moaned for reply.

"Nemmine, we gwine fool dat doctah. Some day we'll th'ow all his nassy medicine 'way, an' he come in an' say: 'Whaih's all my medicine?' Den we answeh up sma't like: 'We done th'owed it out. We don' need no nassy medicine.' Den he look 'roun' an' say: 'Who dat I see runnin' roun' de flo' hyeah, a-lookin' so fat?' an' you up an' say: 'Hit's me, dat's who 'tis, mistah doctor man!' Den he go out an' slam de do' behin' him. Ain' dat fine?"

But the child had closed her eyes, too weak even to listen. So her mother kissed her little thin forehead and tiptoed out, sending in a child from across the hall to take care of Lucy while she was at work, for sick as the little one was she could not stay at home and nurse her.

Hope grasps at a straw, and it was quite in keeping with the condition of Martha's mind that she should open her ears and her heart when they told her of the wonderful works of the faith-cure man. People had gone to him on crutches, and he had touched or rubbed them and they had come away whole. He had gone to the homes of the bed-ridden, and they had risen up to bless him. It was so easy for her to believe it all. The only religion she had ever known, the wild, emotional religion of most of her race, put her credulity to stronger tests than that. Her only question was, would such a man come to her humble room. But she put away even this thought. He must come. She would make him. Already she saw Lucy strong, and running about like a mouse, the joy of her heart and the light of her eyes.

As soon as she could get time she went humbly to see the faith doctor, and laid her case before him, hoping, fearing, trembling.

Yes, he would come. Her heart leaped for joy.

"There is no place," said the faith curist, "too humble for the messenger of heaven to enter. I am following One who went among the humblest and the lowliest, and was not ashamed to be found among publicans and sinners. I will come to your child, madam, and put her again under the law. The law of life is health, and no one who will accept the law need be sick. I am not a physician. I do not claim to be. I only claim to teach people how not to be sick. My fee is five dollars, merely to defray my expenses, that's all. You know the servant is worthy of his hire. And in this little bottle here I have an elixir which has never been known to fail in any of the things claimed for it. Since the world has got used to taking medicine we must make some concessions to its prejudices. But this in reality is not a medicine at all. It is only a symbol. It is really liquefied prayer and faith."

Martha did not understand anything of what he was saying. She did not try to; she did not want to. She only felt a blind trust in him that filled her heart with unspeakable gladness.

Tremulous with excitement, she doled out her poor dollars to him, seized the precious elixir and hurried away home to Lucy, to whom she was carrying life and strength. The little one made a weak attempt to smile at her mother, but the light flickered away and died into greyness on her face.

"Now mammy's little gal gwine to git well fu' sho'. Mammy done bring huh somep'n' good." Awed and reverent, she tasted the wonderful elixir before giving it to the child. It tasted very like sweetened water to her, but she knew that it was not, and had no doubt of its virtues.

Lucy swallowed it as she swallowed everything her mother brought to her. Poor little one! She had nothing to buoy her up or to fight science with.

In the course of an hour her mother gave her the medicine again, and persuaded herself that there was a perceptible brightening in her daughter's face.

Mrs. Mason, Caroline's mother, called across the hall: "How Lucy dis evenin', Mis' Benson?"

"Oh, I think Lucy air right peart," Martha replied. "Come over an' look at huh."

Mrs. Mason came, and the mother told her about the new faith doctor and his wonderful powers.

"Why, Mis' Mason," she said, "'pears like I could see de change in de child de minute she swallowed dat medicine."

Her neighbor listened in silence, but when she went back to her own room it was to shake her head and murmur: "Po' Marfy, she jes' ez blind ez a bat. She jes' go 'long, holdin' on to dat chile wid all huh might, an' I see death in Lucy's face now. Dey ain't no faif nur prayer, nur Jack-leg doctors nuther gwine to save huh."

But Martha needed no pity then. She was happy in her self-delusion.

On the morrow the faith doctor came to see Lucy. She had not seemed so well that morning, even to her mother, who remained at home until the doctor arrived. He carried a conquering air, and a baggy umbrella, the latter of which he laid across the foot of the bed as he bent over the moaning child.

"Give me some brown paper," he commanded.

Martha hastened to obey, and the priestly practitioner dampened it in water and laid it on Lucy's head, all the time murmuring prayers — or were they incantations? — to himself. Then he placed pieces of the paper on the soles of the child's feet and on the palms of her hands, and bound them there.

When all this was done he knelt down and prayed aloud, ending with a peculiar version of the Lord's prayer, supposed to have mystic effect. Martha was greatly impressed, but through it all Lucy lay and moaned.

The faith curist rose to go. "Well, we can look to have her out in a few days. Remember, my good woman, much depends upon you. You must try to keep your mind in a state of belief. Are you saved?"

"Oh, yes, suh. I'm a puffessor," said Martha, and having completed his mission, the man of prayers went out, and Caroline again took Martha's place at Lucy's side.

In the next two days Martha saw, or thought she saw, a steady improvement in Lucy. According to instructions, the brown paper was moved every day, moistened, and put back.

Martha had so far spurred her faith that when she went out on Saturday morning she promised to bring Lucy something good for her Christmas dinner, and a pair of shoes against the time of her going out, and also a little doll. She brought them home that night. Caroline had grown tired and, lighting the lamp, had gone home.

"I done brung my little lady bird huh somep'n nice," said Martha, "here's a lil' doll and de lil' shoes, honey. How's de baby feel?" Lucy did not answer.

"You sleep?" Martha went over to the bed. The little face was pinched and ashen. The hands were cold.

"Lucy! Lucy!" called the mother. "Lucy! Oh, Gawd! It ain't true! She ain't daid! My little one, my las' one!"

She rushed for the elixir and brought it to the bed. The thin dead face stared back at her, unresponsive.

She sank down beside the bed, moaning.

"Daid, daid, oh, my Gawd, gi' me back my chile! Oh, don't I believe you enough? Oh, Lucy, Lucy, my little lamb! I got you yo' gif'. Oh, Lucy!"

The next day was set apart for the funeral. The Mission preacher read: "The Lord giveth and the Lord taketh away, blessed be the name of the Lord," and some one said "Amen!" But Martha could not echo it in her heart. Lucy was her last, her one treasured lamb.

A COUNCIL OF STATE

Luther Hamilton was a great political power. He was neither representative in Congress, senator nor cabinet minister. When asked why he aspired to none of these places of honor and emolument he invariably shrugged his shoulders and smiled inscrutably. In fact, he found it both more pleasant and more profitable simply to boss his party. It gave him power, position and patronage, and yet put him under obligations to no narrow constituency.

As he sat in his private office this particular morning there was a smile upon his face, and his little eyes looked out beneath the heavy grey eyebrows and the massive cheeks with gleams of pleasure. His whole appearance betokened the fact that he was feeling especially good. Even his mail lay neglected before him, and his eyes gazed straight at the wall. What wonder that he should smile and dream. Had he not just the day before utterly crushed a troublesome opponent? Had he not ruined the career of a young man who dared to oppose him, driven him out of public life and forced his business to the wall? If this were not food for self-congratulation pray what is?

Mr. Hamilton's reverie was broken in upon by a tap at the door, and his secretary entered.

"Well, Frank, what is it now? I haven't gone through my mail yet."

"Miss Kirkman is in the outer office, sir, and would like to see you this morning."

"Oh, Miss Kirkman, heh; well, show her in at once."

The secretary disappeared and returned ushering in a young woman, whom the "boss" greeted cordially.

"Ah, Miss Kirkman, good-morning! Good-morning! Always prompt and busy, I see. Have a chair."

Miss Kirkman returned his greeting and dropped into a chair. She began at once fumbling in a bag she carried.

"We'll get right to business," she said. "I know you're busy, and so am I, and I want to get through. I've got to go and hunt a servant for Mrs. Senator Dutton when I leave here."

She spoke in a loud voice, and her words rushed one upon the other as if she were in the habit of saying much in a short space of time. This is a trick of speech frequently acquired by those who visit public men. Miss Kirkman's whole manner indicated bustle and hurry. Even her attire showed it.

She was a plump woman, aged, one would say about thirty. Her hair was brown and her eyes a steely grey — not a bad face, but one too shrewd and aggressive perhaps for a woman. One might have looked at her for a long time and never suspected the truth, that she was allied to the colored race. Neither features, hair nor complexion showed it, but then "colored" is such an elastic word, and Miss Kirkman in reality was colored "for revenue only." She found it more profitable to ally herself to the less important race because she could assume a position among them as a representative woman, which she could never have hoped to gain among the whites. So she was colored, and, without having any sympathy with the people whom she represented, spoke for them and uttered what was supposed by the powers to be the thoughts that were in their breasts.

"Well, from the way you're tossing the papers in that bag I know you've got some news for me."

"Yes, I have, but I don't know how important you'll think it is. Here we are!" She drew forth a paper and glanced at it.

"It's just a memorandum, a list of names of a few men who need watching. The Afro-American convention is to meet on the 22d; that's Thursday of next week. Bishop Carter is to preside. The thing has resolved itself into a fight between those who are office-holders and those who want to be."

"Yes, well what's the convention going to do?"

"They're going to denounce the administration."

"Hem, well in your judgment, what will that amount to, Miss Kirkman?"

"They are the representative talking men from all sections of the country, and they have their following, and so there's no use disputing that they can do some harm."

"Hum, what are they going to denounce the administration for?"

"Oh, there's a spirit of general discontent, and they've got to denounce something, so it had as well be the administration as anything else."

There was a new gleam in Mr. Hamilton's eye that was not one of pleasure as he asked, "Who are the leaders in this movement?"

"That's just what I brought this list for. There's Courtney, editor of the *New York Beacon*, who is rabid; there's Jones of Georgia, Gray of Ohio —"

"Whew," whistled the boss, "Gray of Ohio, why he's on the inside."

"Yes, and I can't see what's the matter with him, he's got his position, and he ought to keep his mouth shut."

"Oh, there are ways of applying the screw. Go on."

"Then, too, there's Shackelford of Mississippi, Duncan of South Carolina, Stowell of Kentucky, and a lot of smaller fry who are not worth mentioning."

"Are they organized?"

"Yes, Courtney has seen to that, the forces are compact."

"We must split them. How is the bishop?"

"Neutral."

"Any influence?"

"Lots of it."

"How's your young man, the one for whom you've been soliciting a place — what's his name?"

Miss Kirkman did her womanhood the credit of blushing, "Joseph Aldrich, you mean. You can trust to me to see that he's on the right side."

"Happy is the man who has the right woman to boss him, and who has sense enough to be bossed by her; his path shall be a path of roses, and his bed a flowery bed of ease. Now to business. They must not denounce the administration. What are the conditions of membership in this convention?"

"Any one may be present, but it costs a fee of five dollars for the privilege of the floor."

Mr. Hamilton turned to the desk and made out a check. He handed it to Miss Kirkman, saying, "Cash this, and pack that convention for the administration. I look to you and the people you may have behind you to check any rash resolutions they may attempt to pass. I want you to be there every day and take notes of the speeches made, and their character and tenor. I shall have Mr. Richardson there also to help you. The record of each man's speech will be sent to his central committee, and we shall know how to treat him in the future. You know, Miss Kirkman, it is our method to help our friends and to crush our enemies. I shall depend upon you to let me know which is which. Good-morning."

"Good-morning, Mr. Hamilton."

"And, oh, Miss Kirkman, just a moment. Frank," the secretary came in, "bring me that jewel case out of the safe. Here, Miss Kirkman, Mrs. Hamilton told me if you came in to ask if you would mind running past the safety deposit vaults and putting these in for her?"

"Certainly not," said Miss Kirkman.

This was one of the ways in which Miss Kirkman was made to remember her race. And the relation to that race, which nothing in her face showed, came out strongly in her willingness thus to serve. The confidence itself flattered her, and she was never tired of telling her acquaintances how she had put such and such a senator's wife's jewels away, or got a servant for a cabinet minister.

When her other duties were done she went directly to a small dingy office building and entered a room, over which was the sign, "Joseph Aldrich, Counselor and Attorney at Law."

"How do, Joe."

"Why, Miss Kirkman, I'm glad to see you," said Mr. Aldrich, coming forward to meet her and setting a chair. He was a slender young man, of a complexion which among the varying shades bestowed among colored people is termed a light brown skin. A mustache and a short Vandyke beard partially covered a mouth inclined to weakness. Looking at them, an observer would have said that Miss Kirkman was the stronger man of the two.

"What brings you out this way today?" questioned Aldrich.

"I'll tell you. You've asked me to marry you, haven't you?"

"Yes."

"Well, I'm going to do it."

"Annie, you make me too happy."

"That's enough," said Miss Kirkman, waving him away. "We haven't any time for romance now. I mean business. You're going to the convention next week."

"Yes."

"And you're going to speak?"

"Of course."

"That's right. Let me see your speech."

He drew a typewritten manuscript from the drawer and handed it to her. She ran her eyes over the pages, murmuring to herself. "Uh, huh, 'wavering, weak, vacilating adminstration, have not given us the protection our rights as citizens demanded — while our brothers were murdered in the South. Nero fiddled while Rome burned, while this modern' — uh, huh, oh, yes, just as I thought," and with a sudden twist Miss Kirkman tore the papers across and pitched them into the grate.

"Miss Kirkman — Annie, what do you mean?"

"I mean that if you're going to marry me, I'm not going to let you go to the convention and kill yourself."

"But my convictions —"

"Look here, don't talk to me about convictions. The colored man is the under dog, and the under dog has no right to have convictions. Listen, you're going to the convention next week and you're going to make a speech, but it won't be that speech. I have just come from Mr. Hamilton's. That convention is to be watched closely. He is to have his people there and they are to take down the words of every man who talks, and these words will be sent to his central committee. The man who goes there with an imprudent tongue goes down. You'd better get to work and see if you can't think of something good the administration has done and dwell on that."

"Whew!"

"Well, I'm off."

"But Annie, about the wedding?"

"Good-morning, we'll talk about the wedding after the convention."

The door closed on her last words, and Joseph Aldrich sat there wondering and dazed at her manner. Then he began to think about the administration. There must be some good things to say for it, and he would find them. Yes, Annie was right — and wasn't she a hustler though?

PART II

It was on the morning of the 22d and near nine o'clock, the hour at which the convention was to be called to order. But Mr. Gray of Ohio had not yet gone in. He stood at the door of the convention hall in deep converse with another man. His companion was a young looking sort of person. His forehead was high and his eyes were keen and alert. The face was mobile and the mouth nervous. It was the face of an enthusiast, a man with deep and intense beliefs, and the boldness or, perhaps, rashness to uphold them.

"I tell you, Gray," he was saying, "it's an outrage, nothing less. Life, liberty, and the pursuit of happiness. Bah! It's all twaddle. Why, we can't even be secure in the first two, how can we hope for the last?"

"You're right, Elkins," said Gray, soberly, "and though I hold a position under the administration, when it comes to a consideration of the wrongs of my race, I cannot remain silent."

"I cannot and will not. I hold nothing from them, and I owe them nothing. I am only a bookkeeper in a commercial house, where their spite cannot reach me, so you may rest assured that I shall not bite my tongue."

"Nor shall I. We shall all be colored men here together, and talk, I hope, freely one to the other. Shall you introduce your resolution today?"

"I won't have a chance unless things move more rapidly than I expect them to. It will have to come up under new business, I should think."

"Hardly. Get yourself appointed on the committee on resolutions."

"Good, but how can I?"

"I'll see to that; I know the bishop pretty well. Ah, good-morning, Miss Kirkman. How do you do, Aldrich?" Gray pursued, turning to the newcomers, who returned his greeting, and passed into the hall.

"That's Miss Kirkman. You've heard of her. She fetches and carries for

Luther Hamilton and his colleagues, and has been suspected of doing some spying, also."

"Who was that with her?"

"Oh, that's her man Friday; otherwise Joseph Aldrich by name, a fellow she's trying to make something of before she marries him. She's got the pull to do it, too."

"Why don't you turn them down?"

"Ah, my boy, you're young, you're young; you show it. Don't you know that a wind strong enough to uproot an oak only ripples the leaves of a creeper against the wall? Outside of the race that woman is really considered one of the leaders, and she trades upon the fact."

"But why do you allow this base deception to go?"

"Because, Elkins, my child," Gray put his hand on the other's shoulder with mock tenderness, "because these seemingly sagacious whites among whom we live are really a very credulous people, and the first one who goes to them with a good front and says 'Look here, I am the leader of the colored people; I am their oracle and prophet,' they immediately exalt and say 'That's so.' Now do you see why Miss Kirkman has a pull?"

"I see, but come on, let's go in; there goes the gavel."

The convention hall was already crowded, and the air was full of the bustle of settling down. When the time came for the payment of their fees, by those who wanted the privilege of the floor, there was a perfect rush for the secretary's desk. Bank notes fluttered everywhere. Miss Kirkman had on a suspiciously new dress and bonnet, but she had done her work well, nevertheless. She looked up into the gallery in a corner that overlooked the stage and caught the eye of a young man who sat there notebook in hand. He smiled, and she smiled. Then she looked over at Mr. Aldrich, who was not sitting with her, and they both smiled complacently. There's nothing like being on the inside.

After the appointment of committees, the genial bishop began his opening address, and a very careful, pretty address it was, too — well worded, well balanced, dealing in broad generalities and studiously saying nothing that would indicate that he had any intention of directing the policy of the meetings. Of course it brought forth all the applause that a bishop's address deserves, and the ladies in the back seats fluttered their fans, and said: "The dear man, how eloquent he is."

Gray had succeeded in getting Elkins placed on the committee on resolutions, but when they came to report, the fiery resolution denouncing the administration for its policy toward the negro was laid on the table. The young man had succeeded in engineering it through the committee, but the chairman decided that its proper place was under the head of new business, where it might be taken up in the discussion of the administration's attitude toward the negro.

"We are here, gentlemen," pursued the bland presiding officer, "to make public sentiment, but we must not try to make it too fast; so if our young friend from Ohio will only hold his resolution a little longer, it will be acted upon at the proper time. We must be moderate and conservative."

Gray sprang to his feet and got the chairman's eye. His face was flushed and he almost shouted: "Conservatism be hanged! We have rolled that word under our tongues when we were being trampled upon; we have preached it in our churches when we were being shot down; we have taught it in our schools when the right to use our learning was denied us, until the very word has come to be a reproach upon a black man's tongue!"

There were cries of "Order! Order!" and "Sit down!" and the gavel was rattling on the chairman's desk. Then some one rose to a point of order, so dear to the heart of the negro debater. The point was sustained and the Ohioan yielded the floor, but not until he had gazed straight into the eyes of Miss Kirkman as they rose from her notebook. She turned red. He curled his lip and sat down, but the blood burned in his face, and it was not the heat of shame, but of anger and contempt that flushed his cheeks.

This outbreak was but the precursor of other storms to follow. Every one had come with an idea to exploit or some proposition to advance. Each one had his panacea for all the aches and pains of his race. Each man who had paid his five dollars wanted his full five dollars' worth of talk. The chairman allowed them five minutes apiece, and they thought time dear at a dollar a minute. But there were speeches to be made for buncombe, and they made the best of the seconds. They howled, they raged, they stormed. They waxed eloquent or pathetic. Jones of Georgia was swearing softly and feelingly into Shackelford's ear. Shackelford was sympathetic and nervous as he fingered a large bundle of manuscript in his back pocket. He got up several times and called "Mr. Chairman," but his voice had been drowned in the tumult. Amid it all, calm and impassive, sat the man, who of all others was expected to be in the heat of the fray.

It had been rumored that Courtney of the *New York Beacon* had come to Washington with blood in his eyes. But there he sat, silent and unmoved, his swarthy, eaglelike face, with its frame of iron-grey hair as unchanging as if he had never had a passionate thought.

"I don't like Jim Courtney's silence," whispered Stowell to a colleague. "There's never so much devil in him as when he keeps still. You look out for him when he does open up."

But all the details of the convention do not belong to this narrative. It is hardly relevant, even, to tell how Stowell's prediction came true, and at the second day's meeting Courtney's calm gave way, and he delivered one of the bitterest speeches of his life. It was in the morning, and he was down for a set speech on "The Negro in the Higher Walks of Life." He started calmly, but as he progressed, the memory of all the wrongs, personal and racial that he had suffered; the knowledge of the disabilities that he and his brethren had to suffer, and the vision of toil unrequited, love rejected, and loyalty ignored, swept him off his feet. He forgot his subject, forgot everything but that he was a crushed man in a crushed race.

The auditors held their breath, and the reporters wrote much.

Turning to them he said, "And to the press of Washington, to whom I have before paid my respects, let me say that I am not afraid to have them take any word that I may say. I came here to meet them on their own ground. I will meet them with pen. I will meet them with pistol," and then raising his tall, spare form, he shouted, "Yes, even though there is but one hundred and thirty-five pounds of me, I will meet them with my fists!"

This was all very rash of Courtney. His paper did not circulate largely, so his real speech, which he printed, was not widely read, while through the columns of the local press, a garbled and distorted version of it went to every corner of the country. Purposely distorted? Who shall say? He had insulted the press; and then Mr. Hamilton was a very wealthy man.

When the time for the consideration of Elkins' resolution came, Courtney, Jones and Shackelford threw themselves body and soul into the fight with Gray and its author. There was a formidable array against them. All the men in office, and all of those who had received even a crumb of promise were for buttering over their wrongs, and making their address to the public a prophecy of better things.

Jones suggested that they send an apology to lynchers for having negroes where they could be lynched. This called for reproof from the other side, and the discussion grew hot and acrimonious. Gray again got the floor, and surprised his colleagues by the plainness of his utterances. Elkins followed him with a biting speech that brought Aldrich to his feet.

Mr. Aldrich had chosen well his time, and had carefully prepared his speech. He recited all the good things that the administration had done, hoped to do, tried to do, or wanted to do, and showed what a very respectable array it was. He counseled moderation and conservatism, and his peroration was a flowery panegyric of the "noble man whose hand is on the helm, guiding the grand old ship of state into safe harbor."

The office-holders went wild with enthusiasm. No self-interest there. The opposition could not argue that this speech was made to keep a job, because the speaker had none. Then Jim Courtney got up and spoiled it all by saying that it may be that the speaker had no job but wanted one.

Aldrich was not moved. He saw a fat salary and Annie Kirkman for him in the near future.

The young lady had done her work well, and when the resolution came to a vote it was lost by a good majority. Aldrich was again on his feet and offering another. The forces of the opposition were discouraged and disorganized, and they made no effort to stop it when the rules were suspended, and it went through on the first reading. Then the convention shouted, that is, part of it did, and Miss Kirkman closed her notebook and glanced up at the gallery again. The young man had closed his book also. Their work was done. The administration had not been denounced, and they had their black-list for Mr. Hamilton's knife.

There were some more speeches made, just so that the talkers should get their money's worth; but for the masses, the convention had lost its interest, and after a few feeble attempts to stir it into life again, a motion to adjourn was entertained. But, before a second appeared, Elkins arose and asked leave to make a statement. It was granted.

"Gentlemen," he said, "we have all heard the resolution which goes to the public as the opinion of the negroes of the country. There are some of us who do not believe that this expresses the feelings of our race, and to us who believe this, Mr. Courtney has given the use of his press in New York, and we shall print our resolution and scatter it broadcast as the minority report of this convention, but the majority report of the race."

Miss Kirkman opened her book again for a few minutes, and then the convention adjourned.

"I wish you'd find out, Miss Kirkman," said Hamilton a couple of days later, "just what firm that young Elkins works for."

"I have already done that. I thought you'd want to know," and she handed him a card.

"Ah, yes," he said. "I have some business relations with that firm. I know them very well. Miss Anderson," he called to his stenographer, "will you kindly take a letter for me. By the way, Miss Kirkman, I have placed Mr. Aldrich. He will have his appointment in a few days."

"Oh, thank you, Mr. Hamilton; is there anything more I can do for you?"

"Nothing. Good-morning."

"Good-morning."

A week later in his Ohio home William Elkins was surprised to be notified by his employers that they were cutting down forces, and would need his services no longer. He wrote at once to his friend Gray to know if there was any chance for him in Washington, and received the answer that Gray could hardly hold his own, as great pressure was being put upon him to force him to resign.

"I think," wrote Gray, "that the same hand is at the bottom of all our misfortunes. This is Hamilton's method."

Miss Kirkman and Mr. Aldrich were married two weeks from the day the convention adjourned. Mr. Gray was removed from his position on account of inefficiency. He is still trying to get back, but the very men to whom his case must go are in the hands of Mr. Hamilton.

SILAS JACKSON

I

Silas Jackson was a young man to whom many opportunities had come. Had he been a less fortunate boy, as his little world looked at it, he might have spent all his days on the little farm where he was born, much as many of his fellows did. But no, Fortune had marked him for her own, and it was destined that he should be known to fame. He was to know a broader field than the few acres which he and his father worked together, and where he and several brothers and sisters had spent their youth.

Mr. Harold Marston was the instrument of Fate in giving Silas his first introduction to the world. Marston, who prided himself on being, besides a man of leisure, something of a sportsman, was shooting over the fields in the vicinity of the Jackson farm. During the week he spent in the region, needing the services of a likely boy, he came to know and like Silas. Upon leaving, he said, "It's a pity for a boy as bright as you are to be tied down in this God-forsaken place. How'd you like to go up to the Springs, Si, and work in a hotel?"

The very thought of going to such a place, and to such work, fired the boy's imagination, although the idea of it daunted him.

"I'd like it powahful well, Mistah Ma'ston," he replied.

"Well, I'm going up there, and the proprietor of one of the best hotels, the Fountain House, is a very good friend of mine, and I'll get him to speak to his head waiter in your behalf. You want to get out of here, and see something of the world, and not stay cooped up with nothing livelier than rabbits, squirrels, and quail."

And so the work was done. The black boy's ambitions that had only needed an encouraging word had awakened into buoyant life. He looked his destiny squarely in the face, and saw that the great world outside beckoned to him. From that time his dreams were eagle-winged. The farm looked narrower to him, the cabin meaner, and the clods were harder to his feet. He learned to hate the plough that he had followed before in dumb content, and there was no longer joy in the woods he knew and loved. Once, out of pure joy of living, he had gone singing about his work; but now, when he sang, it was because his heart was longing for the city of his dreams, and hope inspired the song.

However, after Mr. Marston had been gone for over two weeks, and nothing had been heard from the Springs, the hope died in Silas's heart, and he came to believe that his benefactor had forgotten him. And yet he could not return to the old contentment with his mode of life. Mr. Marston was right, and he was "cooped up there with nothing better than rabbits, squirrels, and quail." The idea had never occurred to him before, but now it struck him with disconcerting force that there was something in him above his surroundings and the labor at which he toiled day by day. He began to see that the cabin was not over clean, and for the first time recognized that his brothers and sisters were positively dirty. He had always looked on it with unconscious eyes before, but now he suddenly developed the capacity for disgust.

When young 'Lishy, noticing his brother's moroseness, attributed it to his strong feeling for a certain damsel, Silas turned on him in a fury. Ambition had even driven out all other feelings, and Dely Manly seemed poor and commonplace to the dark swain, who a month before would have gone any length to gain a smile from her. He compared everything and everybody to the glory of what he dreamed the Springs and its inhabitants to be, and all seemed cheap beside.

Then on a day when his spirits were at their lowest ebb, a passing neighbor handed him a letter which he had found at the little village post office. It was addressed to Mr. Si Jackson, and bore the Springs postmark. Silas was immediately converted from a raw backwoods boy to a man of the world. Save the little notes that had been passed back and forth from boy to girl at the little log schoolhouse where he had gone four fitful sessions, this was his first letter, and it was the first time he had ever been addressed as "Mr." He swelled with a pride that he could not conceal, as with trembling hands he tore the missive open.

He read it through with glowing eyes and a growing sense of his own importance. It was from the head waiter whom Mr. Marston had mentioned, and was couched in the most elegant and high-sounding language. It said that Mr. Marston had spoken for Silas, and that if he came to the Springs, and was quick to learn, "to acquire knowledge," was the head waiter's phrase, a situation would be provided for him. The family gathered around the fortunate son, and gazed on him with awe when he imparted the good news. He became, on the instant, a new being to them. It was as if he had only been loaned to them, and was now being lifted bodily out of their world.

The elder Jackson was a bit doubtful about the matter.

"Of co'se ef you wants to go, Silas, I ain't a-gwine to gainsay you, an' I hope it's all right, but sence freedom dis hyeah piece o' groun's been good enough fu' me, an' I reckon you mought a' got erlong on it."

"But pap, you see it's diff'ent now. It's diff'ent, all I wanted was a chanst."

"Well, I reckon you got it, Si, I reckon you got it."

The younger children whispered long after they had gone to bed that night, wondering and guessing what the great place to which brother Si was going could be like, and they could only picture it as like the great white-domed city whose picture they had seen in the gaudy Bible foisted upon them by a passing agent.

As for Silas, he read and reread the letter by the light of a tallow dip until he was too sleepy to see, and every word was graven on his memory; then he went to bed with the precious paper under his pillow. In spite of his drowsiness, he lay awake for some time, gazing with heavy eyes into the darkness, where he saw the great city and his future; then he went to sleep to dream of it.

From then on, great were the preparations for the boy's departure. So little happened in that vicinity that the matter became a neighborhood event, and the black folk for three miles up and down the road manifested their interest in Silas's good fortune.

"I hyeah you gwine up to de Springs," said old Hiram Jones, when he met the boy on the road a day or two before his departure.

"Yes, suh, I's gwine up thaih to wo'k in a hotel. Mistah Ma'ston, he got me the job."

The old man reined in his horse slowly, and deposited the liquid increase of a quid of tobacco before he said; "I hyeah tell it's powahful wicked up in dem big cities."

"Oh, I reckon I ain't a-goin' to do nuffin wrong. I's goin' thaih to wo'k."

"Well, you has been riz right," commented the old man doubtfully, "but den, boys will be boys."

He drove on, and the prospect of a near view of wickedness did not make the Springs less desirable in the boy's eyes. Raised as he had been, almost away from civilization, he hardly knew the meaning of what the world called wickedness. Not that he was strong or good. There had been no occasion for either quality to develop; but that he was simple and primitive, and had been close to what was natural and elemental. His faults and sins were those of the gentle barbarian. He had not yet learned the subtler vices of a higher civilization.

Silas, however, was not without the pride of his kind, and although his father protested that it was a useless extravagance, he insisted upon going to the nearest village and investing part of his small savings in a new suit of clothes. It was quaint and peculiar apparel, but it was the boy's first "store suit," and it filled him with unspeakable joy. His brothers and sisters regarded his new magnificence with envying admiration. It would be a long while before they got away from bagging, homespun, and copperas-colored cotton, whacked out into some semblance of garments by their "mammy." And so, armed with a light bundle, in which were his few other belongings, and fearfully and wonderfully arrayed, Silas Jackson set out for the Springs. His father's parting injunctions were ringing in his ears, and the memory of his mammy's wet eyes and sad face lingered in his memory. She had wanted him to take the gaudy Bible away, but it was too heavy to carry, especially as he was to walk the whole thirty miles to the land of promise. At the last, his feeling of exaltation gave way to one of sorrow, and as he went down the road, he turned often to look at the cabin, until it faded from sight around the bend. Then a lump rose in his throat, and he felt like turning and running back to it. He had never thought the old place could seem so dear. But he kept his face steadily forward and trudged on toward his destiny.

The Springs was the fashionable resort of Virginia, where the aristocrats who thought they were ill went to recover their health and to dance. Compared with large cities of the North, it was but a small town, even including the transient population, but in the eyes of the rural blacks and the poor whites of the region, it was a place of large importance.

Hither, on the morning after his departure from the home gate, came Silas Jackson, a little foot-sore and weary, but hopeful withal. In spite of the pains that he had put upon his dressing, he was a quaint figure on the city streets. Many an amused smile greeted him as he went his way, but he saw them not. Inquiring the direction, he kept on, until the many windows and broad veranda of the great hotel broke on his view, and he gasped in amazement and awe at the sight of it, and a sudden faintness seized him. He was reluctant to go on, but the broad grins with which some colored men who were working about the place regarded him, drove him forward, in spite of his embarrassment.

He found his way to the kitchen, and asked in trembling tones for the head waiter. Breakfast being over, that individual had leisure to come to the kitchen. There, with the grinning waiters about him, he stopped and calmly surveyed Silas. He was a very pompous head waiter.

Silas had never been self-conscious before, but now he became distressfully aware of himself — of his awkwardness, of his clumsy feet and dangling hands, of the difference between his clothes and the clothes of the men about him.

After a survey, which seemed to the boy of endless duration, the head waiter spoke, and his tone was the undisputed child of his looks.

"I pussoom," said Mr. Buckner, "that you are the pusson Mistah Ma'ston spoke to the p'op'ietor about?"

"Yes, suh, I reckon I is. He p'omised to git me a job up hyeah, an' I got yo' lettah —" here Silas, who had set his bundle on the floor in coming into the Presence, began to fumble in his pockets for the letter. He searched long in vain, because his hands trembled, and he was nervous under the eyes of this great personage who stood unmoved and looked calmly at him.

Finally the missive was found and produced, though not before the perspiration was standing thick on Silas's brow. The head waiter took the sheet.

"Ve'y well, suh, ve'y well. You are evidently the p'oper pusson, as I reco'nize this as my own chirography."

The up-country boy stood in awed silence. He thought he had never heard such fine language before.

"I ca'culate that you have nevah had no experience in hotel work," pursued Mr. Buckner somewhat more graciously.

"I's nevah done nuffin' but wo'k on a farm; but evahbody 'lows I's right handy." The fear that he would be sent back home without employment gave him boldness.

"I see, I see," said the head waiter. "Well, we'll endeavor to try an' see how soon you can learn. Mistah Smith, will you take this young man in charge, an' show him how to get about things until we are ready to try him in the dinin'-room?"

A rather pleasant-faced yellow boy came over to Silas and showed him where to put his things and what to do.

"I guess it'll be a little strange at first, if you've never been a hotel man, but you'll ketch on. Just you keep your eye on me."

All that day as Silas blundered about slowly and awkwardly, he looked with wonder and admiration at the ease and facility with which his teacher and the other men did their work. They were so calm, so precise, and so self-sufficient. He wondered if he would ever be like them, and felt very hopeless as the question presented itself to him.

They were a little prone to laugh at him, but he was so humble and so sensible that he thought he must be laughable; so he laughed a little shame-facedly at himself, and only tried the harder to imitate his companions. Once when he dropped a dish upon the floor, he held his breath in consternation, but when he found that no one paid any attention to it, he picked it up and went his way.

He was tired that night, more tired than ploughing had ever made him, and was thankful when Smith proposed to show him at once to the rooms apportioned to the servants. Here he sank down and fell into a doze as soon as his companion left him with the remark that he had some studying to do. He found afterward that Smith was only a temporary employee at the

Springs, coming there during the vacations of the school which he attended, in order to eke out the amount which it cost him for his education. Silas thought this a very wonderful thing at first, but when he grew wiser, as he did finally, he took the point of view of most of his fellows and thought that Smith was wasting both time and opportunities.

It took a very short time for Silas's unfamiliarity with his surroundings to wear off, and for him to become acquainted with the duties of his position. He grew at ease with his work, and became a favorite both in dining-room and kitchen. Then began his acquaintance with other things, and there were many other things at the Springs which an unsophisticated young man might learn.

Silas's social attainments were lamentably sparse, but being an apt youngster, he began to acquire them, quite as he acquired his new duties, and different forms of speech. He learned to dance — almost a natural gift of the negro — and he was introduced into the subtleties of flirtation. At first he was a bit timid with the nurse-girls and maids whom the wealthy travelers brought with them, but after a few lessons from very able teachers, he learned the manly art of ogling to his own satisfaction, and soon became as proficient as any of the other black coxcombs.

If he ever thought of Dely Manly any more, it was with a smile that he had been able at one time to consider her seriously. The people at home, be it said to his credit, he did not forget. A part of his wages went back every month to help better the condition of the cabin. But Silas himself had no desire to return, and at the end of a year he shuddered at the thought of it. He was quite willing to help his father, whom he had now learned to call the "old man," but he was not willing to go back to him.

II

Early in his second year at the Springs Marston came for a stay at the hotel. When he saw his protégé, he exclaimed: "Why, that isn't Si, is it?"

"Yes, suh," smiled Silas.

"Well, well, well, what a change. Why, boy, you've developed into a regular fashion-plate. I hope you're not advertising for any of the Richmond tailors. They're terrible Jews, you know."

"You see, a man has to be neat aroun' the hotel, Mistah Ma'ston."

"Whew, and you've developed dignity, too. By the Lord Harry, if I'd have made that remark to you about a year and a half ago, there at the cabin, you'd have just grinned. Ah, Silas, I'm afraid for you. You've grown too fast. You've gained a certain poise and ease at the expense of — of — I don't know what, but something that I liked better. Down there at home you were just a plain darky. Up here you are trying to be like me, and you are colored."

"Of co'se, Mistah Ma'ston," said Silas politely, but deprecatingly, "the worl' don't stan' still."

"Platitudes — the last straw!" exclaimed Mr. Marston tragically. "There's an old darky preacher up at Richmond who says it does, and I'm sure I think more of his old fog-horn blasts than I do of your parrot tones. Ah! Si, this is the last time that I shall ever fool with good raw material. However, don't let this bother you. As I remember, you used to sing well. I'm going to have some of my friends up at my rooms tonight; get some of the boys together, and come and sing for us. And remember, nothing hifalutin; just the same old darky songs you used to sing."

"All right, suh, we'll be up."

Silas was very glad to be rid of his old friend, and he thought when Marston had gone that he was, after all, not such a great man as he had believed. But the decline in his estimation of Mr. Marston's importance did not deter him from going that night with three of his fellow-waiters to sing for that gentleman. Two of the quartet insisted upon singing fine music, in order to show their capabilities, but Silas had received his cue, and held out for the old songs. Silas Jackson's tenor voice rang out in the old plantation melodies with the force and feeling that old memories give. The concert was a great success, and when Marston pressed a generous-sized bank-note into his hand that night, he whispered, "Well, I'm glad there's one thing you haven't lost, and that's your voice."

That was the beginning of Silas's supremacy as manager and first tenor of the Fountain Hotel Quartet, and he flourished in that capacity for two years longer; then came Mr. J. Robinson Frye, looking for talent, and Silas, by reason of his prominence, fell in this way.

Mr. J. Robinson Frye was an educated and enthusiastic young mulatto gentleman, who, having studied music abroad, had made art his mistress. As well as he was able, he wore the shock of hair which was the sign manual of his profession. He was a plausible young man of large ideas, and had composed some things of which the critics had spoken well. But the chief trouble with his work was that his one aim was money. He did not love the people among whom American custom had placed him, but he had respect for their musical ability.

"Why," he used to exclaim in the sudden bursts of enthusiasm to which he was subject, "why, these people are the greatest singers on earth. They've got more emotion and more passion than any other people, and they learn easier. I could take a chorus of forty of them, and with two months' training make them sing the roof off the Metropolitan Opera house."

When Mr. Frye was in New York, he might be seen almost any day at the piano of one or the other of the negro clubs, either working at some new inspiration, or playing one of his own compositions, and all black clubdom looked on him as a genius.

His latest scheme was the training of a colored company which should do a year's general singing throughout the country, and then having acquired poise and a reputation, produce his own opera.

It was for this he wanted Silas, and in spite of the warning and protests of friends, Silas went with him to New York, for he saw his future loom large before him.

The great city frightened him at first, but he found there some, like himself, drawn from the smaller towns of the South. Others in the company were the relics of the old days of negro minstrelsy, and still others recruited from the church choirs in the large cities. Silas was an adaptable fellow, but it seemed a little hard to fall in with the ways of his new associates. Most of them seemed as far away from him in their knowledge of worldly things as had the waiters at the Springs a few years before. He was half afraid of the chorus girls, because they seemed such different beings from the nurse girls down home. However, there was little time for moping or regrets. Mr. Frye was, it must be said, an indefatigable worker. They were rehearsing every day. Silas felt himself learning to sing. Meanwhile, he knew that he was learning other things — a few more elegancies and vices. He looked upon the "rounders" with admiration and determined to be one. So, after rehearsals were over other occupations held him. He came to be known at the clubs and was quite proud of it, and he grew bolder with the chorus girls, because he was to be a star.

After three weeks of training, the company opened, and Silas, who had never sung anything heavier than "Bright Sparkles in the Churchyard," was dressed in a Fauntleroy suit, and put on to sing in a scene from "Rigoletto."

Every night he was applauded to the echo by "the unskilful," until he came to believe himself a great singer. This belief was strengthened when the girl who performed the Spanish dance bestowed her affections upon him. He was very happy and very vain, and for the first time he forgot the people down in a little old Virginia cabin. In fact, he had other uses for his money.

For the rest of the season, either on the road or in and about New York, he sang steadily. Most of the things for which he had longed and had striven had come to him. He was known as a rounder, his highest ambition. His waistcoats were the loudest to be had. He was possessed of a factitious ease and self-possession that was almost aggression. The hot breath of the city had touched and scorched him, and had dried up within him whatever was good and fresh. The pity of it was that he was proud of himself, and utterly unconscious of his own degradation. He looked upon himself as a man of the world, a fine product of the large opportunities of a great city.

Once in those days he heard of Smith, his old-time companion at the Springs. He was teaching at some small place in the South. Silas laughed contemptuously when he heard how his old friend was employed. "Poor fellow," he said, "what a pity he didn't come up here, and make something out of himself, instead of starving down there on little or nothing," and he mused on how much better his fate had been.

The season ended. After a brief period of rest, the rehearsals for Frye's opera were begun. Silas confessed to himself that he was tired; he had a cough, too, but Mr. Frye was still enthusiastic, and this was to be the great triumph, both for the composer and the tenor.

"Why, I tell you, man," said Frye, "it's going to be the greatest success of the year. I am the only man who has ever put grand-opera effects into comic opera with success. Just listen to the chords of this opening chorus." And so he inspired the singer with some of his own spirit. They went to work with a will. Silas might have been reluctant as he felt the strain upon him grow, but that he had spent all his money, and Frye, as he expressed it, was "putting up for him," until the opening of the season.

Then one day he was taken sick, and although Frye fumed, the rehearsals had to go on without him. For awhile his companions came to see him, and then they gradually ceased to come. So he lay for two months. Even Sadie, his dancing sweetheart, seemed to have forgotten him. One day he sent for her, but the messenger returned to say she could not come, she was busy. She had married the man with whom she did a turn at the roof-garden. The news came, too, that the opera had been abanboned, and that Mr. Frye had taken out a company with a new tenor, whom he pronounced far superior to the former one.

Silas gazed blankly at the wall. The hollowness of his life all came suddenly before him. All his false ideals crumbled, and he lay there with nothing to hope for. Then came back the yearnings for home, for the cabin and the fields, and there was no disgust in his memory of them.

When his strength partly returned, he sold some of the few things that remained to him from his prosperous days, and with the money purchased a ticket for home; then spent, broken, hopeless, all contentment and simplicity gone, he turned his face toward his native fields.

ACCOUNTABILITY

Folks ain't got no right to censuah othah folks about dey habits;
  Him dat giv' de squir'ls de bushtails made de bobtails fu' de rabbits.
Him dat built de gread big mountains hollered out de little valleys,
  Him dat made de streets an' driveways wasn't shamed to make de alleys.

We is all constructed diff'ent, d'ain't no two of us de same;
  We cain't he'p ouah likes an' dislikes, ef we'se bad we ain't to blame.
Ef we'se good, we need n't show off, case you bet it ain't ouah doin'
  We gits into su'ttain channels dat we jes' cain't he'p pu'suin'.

But we all fits into places dat no othah ones could fill,
  An' we does the things we has to, big er little, good er ill.
John cain't tek de place o' Henry, Su an' Sally ain't alike;
  Bass ain't nuthin' like a suckah, chub ain't nuthin' like a pike.

When you come to think about it, how it's all planned out it's splendid.
  Nuthin's done er evah happens, 'dout hit's somefin' dat's intended;
Don't keer whut you does, you has to, an' hit sholy beats de dickens,—
  Viney, go put on de kittle, I got one o' mastah's chickens.

CHRISTMAS CAROL

Ring out, ye bells!
All Nature swells
With gladness at the wondrous story, —
The world was at lorn,
But Christ is born
To change our sadness into glory.

Sing, earthlings, sing!
To-night a King
Hath come from heaven's high throne to bless us.
The outstretched hand
O'er all the land
Is raised in pity to caress us.

Come at His call;
Be joyful all;
Away with mourning and with sadness!
The heavenly choir
With holy fire
Their voices raise in songs of gladness.

The darkness breaks
And Dawn awakes,
Her cheeks suffused with youthful blushes.
The rocks and stones
In holy tones
Are singing sweeter than the thrushes.

Then why should we
In silence be,
When Nature lends her voice to praises;
When heaven and earth
Proclaim the truth
Of Him for whom that lone star blazes?

No, be not still,
But with a will
Strike all your harps and set them ringing;
On hill and heath
Let every breath
Throw all its power into singing!

THE HAUNTED OAK

Pray why are you so bare, so bare,
Oh, bough of the old oak-tree;
And why, when I go through the shade you throw,
Runs a shudder over me?

My leaves were green as the best, I trow,
And sap ran free in my veins,
But I saw in the moonlight dim and weird
A guiltless victim's pains.

I bent me down to hear his sigh;
I shook with his gurgling moan,
And I trembled sore when they rode away,
And left him here alone.

They'd charged him with the old, old crime,
And set him fast in jail:
Oh, why does the dog howl all night long,
And why does the night wind wail?

He prayed his prayer and he swore his oath,
And he raised his hand to the sky;
But the beat of hoofs smote on his ear,
And the steady tread drew nigh.

Who is it rides by night, by night,
Over the moonlit road?
And what is the spur that keeps the pace,
What is the galling goad?

And now they beat at the prison door,
"Ho, keeper, do not stay!
We are friends of him whom you hold within,
And we fain would take him away

"From those who ride fast on our heels
With mind to do him wrong;
They have no care for his innocence,
And the rope they bear is long."

They have fooled the jailer with lying words,
They have fooled the man with lies;
The bolts unbar, the locks are drawn,
And the great door open flies.

Now they have taken him from the jail,
  And hard and fast they ride,
And the leader laughs low down in his throat,
  As they halt my trunk beside.

Oh, the judge, he wore a mask of black,
  And the doctor one of white,
And the minister, with his oldest son,
  Was curiously bedight.

Oh, foolish man, why weep you now?
  'Tis but a little space,
And the time will come when these shall dread
  The mem'ry of your face.

I feel the rope against my bark,
  And the weight of him in my grain,
I feel in the throe of his final woe
  The touch of my own last pain.

And never more shall leaves come forth
  On the bough that bears the ban;
I am burned with dread, I am dried and dead,
  From the curse of a guiltless man.

And ever the judge rides by, rides by,
  And goes to hunt the deer,
And ever another rides his soul
  In the guise of a mortal fear.

And ever the man he rides me hard,
  And never a night stays he;
For I feel his curse as a haunted bough,
  On the trunk of a haunted tree.

HE HAD HIS DREAM

He had his dream, and all through life,
Worked up to it through toil and strife.
Afloat fore'er before his eyes,
It colored for him all his skies:
     The storm-cloud dark
     Above his bark,
The calm and listless vault of blue
Took on its hopeful hue,
It tinctured every passing beam —
     He had his dream.

He labored hard and failed at last,
His sails too weak to bear the blast,
The raging tempests tore away
And sent his beating bark astray.
     But what cared he
     For wind or sea!
He said, "The tempest will be short,
My bark will come to port."
He saw through every cloud a gleam —
     He had his dream.

THE POET AND HIS SONG

A song is but a little thing,
And yet what joy it is to sing!
In hours of toil it gives me zest,
And when at eve I long for rest;
When cows come home along the bars,
    And in the fold I hear the bell,
As Night, the shepherd, herds his stars,
    I sing my song, and all is well.

There are no ears to hear my lays,
No lips to lift a word of praise;
But still, with faith unfaltering,
I live and laugh and love and sing.
What matters yon unheeding throng?
    They cannot feel my spirit's spell,
Since life is sweet and love is long,
    I sing my song, and all is well.

My days are never days of ease;
I till my ground and prune my trees.
When ripened gold is all the plain,
I put my sickle to the grain.
I labor hard, and toil and sweat,
    While others dream within the dell;
But even while my brow is wet,
    I sing my song, and all is well.

Sometimes the sun, unkindly hot,
My garden makes a desert spot;
Sometimes a blight upon the tree
Takes all my fruit away from me;
And then with throes of bitter pain
    Rebellious passions rise and swell;
But — life is more than fruit or grain,
    And so I sing, and all is well.